The End of the Dreams

JAMES GUNN

THE END OF
THE DREAMS

THREE SHORT NOVELS
about Space, Happiness, and Immortality

NEW YORK

CHARLES SCRIBNER'S SONS

Copyright © 1975 James Gunn

Library of Congress Cataloging in Publication Data

Gunn, James E 1923–
    The end of the dreams.

    CONTENTS: Space is a lonely place.—The joy ride.
—The immortal.
    I. Title.
PZ3.G9526En [PS3513.U797]   813'.5'4   75–12887
ISBN 0–684–14352–6

"Space is a Lonely Place" originally appeared in Venture Science Fiction, Copyright 1957 Fantasy House, Inc., and was part of *Station in Space* published by Bantam Books in 1958.

"The Joy Ride" originally appeared in *Startling Stories*, Copyright © 1955 by Standard Magazines, Inc., and was reprinted as "The Naked Sky" in *The Joy Makers*, published by Bantam Books in 1961.

"The Immortal" originally appeared in *Star Science Fiction #4*, Copyright 1958 by Ballantine Books, Inc., and was part of *The Immortals* published by Bantam Books in 1962.

1 3 5 7 9 11 13 15 17 19 **H/C** 20 18 16 14 12 10 8 6 4 2

Printed in the United States of America

To Bill and Margie Bowers

Contents

Introduction

I have trouble with my dreams.

This is a shameful thing that I have never told anyone before, not even my wife.

I don't mean that I have trouble dreaming. As far as I know, I dream as much as anyone. My problem is that my dreams never come out the way they should, the way I imagine everyone else's do, with the dreamer getting in his dreams what he often cannot get in real life. Gratification—without guilt or interruption.

My dreams aren't like that. If I dream about a feast, I never get to eat it. If I dream about a contest, something almost always happens to keep me from winning—or if I should chance to win, to keep me from enjoying it.

Since I have spent a substantial portion of my life in and around schools and colleges, some of my persistent dreams have to do with going to school. Those dreams may be the worst: I show up late for an important class, or remember at the end of the semester that I enrolled in a class I've never attended. These dreams are filled with panic, in spite of the fact that for many years I have been on the side of the desk where the roll is taken and the records are kept, and in spite of the fact that today's students think no more of missing a class or a whole semester than they think of skipping a haircut.

Well, all these could be dismissed as the normal nightmares everyone has occasionally, but I have them all the time. Even if I have a romantic dream, someone or something always breaks up an intimate situation at the most inopportune moment.

The Freudians would say that I have an overpunitive superego which won't allow me to enjoy what I haven't earned, even when I'm asleep and it's just immaterial dreamstuff. But I've begun to wonder lately if a subconscious mind or an overactive superego that keeps putting up obstacles in the way of wishes may be useful, perhaps even essential, to the writer of fiction. Most fiction is about people who want something and can't get it, one way or another, and the most interesting fiction is about people with unusual desires or unique difficulties in achieving them— that is, about trouble with dreams.

Last year Charles Scribner's Sons published a collection containing four of my stories under the title of *Some Dreams Are Nightmares.* The title comes from a statement the late John W. Campbell, longtime editor of *Analog,* once made about science fiction: "Fiction is simply dreams written out. Science fiction consists of the hopes and dreams and fears (for some dreams are nightmares) of a technically based society."

Some of men's dreams are nightmares. Some start out as nightmares, and others turn into nightmares. The ones I dealt with in my previous book—immortality, happiness, the conquest of space—have turned into nightmares.

In this book I present the end of those dreams, three short novels that continue and conclude the dreams begun in last year's book: "Space Is a Lonely Place," "The Joy Ride," and "The Immortal."

I've talked about dreams; now I wish to devote a few words to ends.

Eschatology, according to my dictionary, is a theological term which refers to "the doctrine of the last or final things, as death, resurrection, immortality, the end of the age, the second advent of Christ, judgment, and the future state." I don't know what these matters bring to your mind, but to me—with the possible exception of the Second Coming—they sound like subjects for science fiction. They are important matters, and many people no longer look to theology for answers; so science fiction, which often has a religious quality, has taken up the task of the speculative medieval monk.

Last things are one of man's dreams whose fulfillment, if it is ever achieved, lies in the future; they are the proper subject of science fiction, which deals with both dreams and the future. In its main current, science fiction has preached a kind of secular religion including as its tenets faith in man as the measure of all things and faith in his ultimate goal, which is to understand the universe; and today, science fiction may provide the only believable dialogue about death, resurrection, immortality, and the end of our way of life, or of civilization, or of man himself, as well as the larger issues involving the end of the earth, of the solar system, of the galaxy, and of the universe.

C. S. Lewis, I think, was the first to apply the term "eschatology" to science fiction, labeling it a subspecies (his other subspecies are displaced persons, engineers, speculative science, and imaginative delight in beauty or the wonderful). In his essay "On Science Fiction" (in *Of Other Worlds,* New York: Harcourt, Brace and World, 1966), he went on to describe the value of eschatological science fiction: "Work of this kind gives expression to thoughts and emotions which I think it good that we should sometimes entertain. It is sobering and cathartic to remember, now and then, our collective smallness, our apparent isolation, the apparent indifference of nature, the slow, biological, geological, and astronomical processes which may, in the long run, make many of our hopes (possibly some of our fears) ridiculous. If *memento mori* is sauce for the individual, I do not know why the species should be spared the taste of it."

In its pursuit of last things, science fiction has developed a love affair with ultimates. Bigger and better—the belief in progress— inevitably evolve into biggest and best, which is not progress but dream. When the dream is dealt with in ways that are not intended to convince the reader of its possibility, the story is myth or fairy tale or fantasy; when it is translated into the real world, where causality operates, it is science fiction.

Over the some one hundred to one hundred and fifty years that science fiction has been written, stories have dealt with such dreams as the mightiest machine, the ultimate metal, the perfect mirror, the biggest telescope, and the greatest microscope. Science fiction hungers to see the infinite, from the infinitesimally small to the edges of the universe, and from the beginning of things to their final end.

Like science fiction, men have a talent for simplifying existence. Perhaps it is the only way they can handle the great and confusing variety of life, which apparently has no order except that which man chooses to enforce upon it; and so men categorize phenomena and sometimes make the mistake of believing that their categories represent reality instead of a convenience. They say—and we distrust them for saying—"There are only two kinds of people in this world. . . ."

Science fiction, however, being not only eschatological but popular, tends to simplify even more. Like an experiment in the behavioral sciences, it attempts to keep all factors constant except one and to predict how that one will develop. It deals with the purified situation, stripped of its extraneous encumbrances; matters get boiled down to essential qualities, issues to their elemental forms, and people to those qualities they must have to deal with those issues.

To accomplish this end, science fiction writers must dispense with some of the luxuries of the mainstream, whose authors are free to display the diversity of existence and the complexity of character. Some critics mistake this characteristic of science fiction stories for a basic inferiority in form or a deficiency in execution; but it is the essence of the genre. On this point, Lewis commented:

It is absurd to condemn them because they do not often display any deep or sensitive characterization. They oughtn't to. It is a fault if they do. . . . Every good writer knows that the more unusual the scenes and events of his story are, the slighter, the more ordinary, the more typical his persons should be. Hence Gulliver is a commonplace little man and Alice a commonplace little girl. If they had been more remarkable they would have wrecked their books. . . . To tell how odd things struck odd people is to have an oddity too much: he who is to see strange things must not himself be strange. He ought to be as nearly as possible Everyman or Anyman.

All of which is apologetic preface to the statement that science fiction can be divided into two types: stories that extrapolate from current trends, and stories that develop from an unusual event; the two kinds of stories have been called, more simply, "if this goes on . . ." and "what if," which also happen to be the titles of stories by Robert Heinlein and Isaac Asimov, respectively. Having oversimplified, let me quickly add that most stories are blends of the two types: in even the most extrapolative of stories one may find elements of the "what if." And in even the most speculative of stories, there are aspects of extrapolation.

But since any taxonomy is only a means of ordering experience, let me apply my dichotomy to the stories in this book. "Space Is a Lonely Place" is the conclusion of the related stories published as *Station in Space*, a book that began with a story called "The Cave of Night." I had just written a couple of space epics and had decided that science fiction was getting too far from the present, that readers, particularly readers who had never been initiated into the mysteries of science fiction and all its shared assumptions, could relate better to events in the immediate future. I set about to dramatize the future events in the coming conquest of space.

I was right in one sense: "The Cave of Night" was selected for

THE END OF THE DREAMS

a best-of-the-year anthology and was dramatized twice, once on NBC radio's "X Minus One" and again as an hour-long television play on the old "Desilu Playhouse" under the title of "Man in Orbit," featuring Lee Marvin and E. G. Marshall. But I also encountered problems: events are likely to catch up with extrapolations, and so it proved with "The Cave of Night." "Space Is a Lonely Place," however, is still possible, still relevant. It is, in a sense, an extrapolation; but because of the way it deals with man's long-held dream of traveling to another world, it is a mythopoeic story, and perhaps eschatological as well.

"The Joy Ride," on the other hand, is pure eschatology, dealing not only with ultimate happiness but with the nature of reality itself. It is the continuation and conclusion of the history of hedonics—the science of happiness—described in "The Hedonist," which was the central portion of *The Joy Makers*. "The Hedonist" described a society in which happiness is the only good and government is charged with responsibility for the happiness of every citizen. What happens after everyone is happy might seem like anticlimax, but it is only the beginning of "The Joy Ride."

"The Immortal" continues and concludes the story of one immortal man and the people who want his blood to make them young again, which began in "New Blood" and continued as the story of society's reaction to the fact of immortality in "Medic." "New Blood" was the basis for an ABC-TV "Movie of the Week" in 1969 and the 1970 television series, both called "The Immortal." Television would never have dealt with my "Immortal," however, not with its implied criticism of medicine and its variety of ways to achieve immortality, not all of them pretty and not all their results desirable. Part extrapolation, part eschatology, "The Immortal" considers whether man is ready to pay the price for immortality. For everything has its price.

The End of the Dreams begins where *Some Dreams Are Nightmares* left off. It tells how the dreams end, and if the stories continue after the last page is turned, why that's often the way with dreams. Dreams never really end; the dreamer just wakes up.

JAMES GUNN
Lawrence, Kansas

Space Is
a Lonely Place

I

TERRY PHILLIPS watched her husband come out of the bedroom brushing down his graying hair. It wouldn't lie right after it was washed, even though Lloyd tried to tame it with a stocking cap. The one-third gravity did that.

She studied him with eyes cleared for a moment of ten years' habit. Those ten years had aged Lloyd more than they should. He looked much older than a man still this side of forty. His face was dark and marred by frown and squint lines. His eyes were flecked with cataracts. He was thinner. But he was still a handsome man, almost as handsome as when he had stood with her in their marriage ceremony.

There were unpleasant memories, too, but she wouldn't think of those. Not now. Not when her mind was made up.

Lloyd was worried. She wondered if it was the ship.

But the first thing he asked about was the children.

Terry laughed. She could still laugh. "Paul and Carl have been up for hours. It's ten o'clock, sleepy head. They're in the recreation room."

"Oh. Fine. Fine." He rubbed his chin absently and stared at the rungs of the metal ladder fixed against the inner wall. They mounted toward a square door in the convex ceiling. It was closed. Something thumped against it; they heard muffled laughter.

Terry said gently, "Breakfast is ready."

Lloyd started. "Oh. Yes." He sat down and drained his glass

3

of reconstituted orange juice. He started in on the artificial eggs as if he really enjoyed them. "I got in late last night. After one. Didn't wake you, did I?"

Terry lied. "No. Were the tapes bad again?"

Lloyd nodded, frowning. "Two hundred and fifty-nine days. If they can hold out one day longer, they'll make it. They'll be the first men to complete a successful trip to Mars. They've got to hold out!"

She said slowly, "I think you must be the most cold-blooded man I've ever known. Those men are friends of yours, and you care more about the success of the trip than whether they live or die."

Lloyd sipped the instant coffee. "You think I wouldn't have traded places with any of them? They knew what they were doing. They knew that two previous attempts had failed. They went out with their eyes open.

"What do you think it's like to be in the viewing room, watching them walk to the brink of madness and lean over, and know that they're God-knows-how-many million miles away, and you can't do a thing?"

"I'm sorry. Forget it."

Lloyd looked at her quickly. "You aren't really sorry, are you?" He paused. "I've decided to get scooters for the kids on their birthdays."

Terry put down the cup she had been holding in both hands as if to warm them. "Lloyd! Carl's just six, and Paul's only eight."

"You can't keep them cooped up in these six rooms forever. They're responsible kids. It's perfectly safe."

Terry said with iron-hard determination, "They'll never use them." Her lips were compressed into thin, pale lines. "You might as well know. I'm leaving you. I'm taking the children with me. I wasn't going to tell you while you were worried about the *Santa Maria*, but we can't go on like this any longer."

"Terry!" Lloyd's eyes were shocked and hurt. "I know I'm

hard to live with, but I'm no worse than I ever was. You know I couldn't live without you and the kids. You're my wife—"

Terry shook her head. "You're married to that Wheel out there. You're mother to those men. You don't need a wife. I don't know why I ever thought I could make it work. I must have been crazy. Everyone said I was crazy to come out here with you.

"I've been living in this stupid ball for ten years. It stinks, Lloyd, literally stinks. Old sweat and old food and oil. If I fry onions I can smell them for weeks. The air is so wet and thick you can almost feel it like damp cotton in your lungs. I want to feel like a human being again. I'm going Inside, Lloyd. I'm never coming out again." Her voice was close to hysteria. "Never!"

Lloyd said quickly, "But there are other women out here now. This is a permanent base. We're space dwellers. You can't expect us to live without families—"

"Women can't live out here, Lloyd!" Terry tried to control her voice. "The other women are hermits, just like me. How long has it been since you saw one of them outside her cocoon? When we get together, it's by television. Did you ever try to play bridge by television? I haven't seen another woman in the flesh for a year."

Lloyd's voice was suddenly sober. "Have you thought about the kids?"

"That's all I have thought about. Do you know those children have never been on Earth? Never? They're being cheated of their birthright—blue skies and green grass and playing baseball with the other kids. They'll never be human beings." She was screaming now. "They're growing up into monsters! Monsters!"

Lloyd looked at her, not moving, not saying anything. "I think they're pretty darned nice kids. Don't project your disappointments into them, Terry. Children don't see things the way we do. As long as they have love and security—"

She was panting with the effort to control herself.

Lloyd said gently, "Maybe you need a vacation. We can afford it."

"Another one? Without the children? No, thanks. When I leave it will be for good, and the children will go with me."

Lloyd's face grew tight. He bit his lower lip the way he did when he tried to suppress his emotion. *If he'd only let it out,* Terry thought. *Just once. So I wouldn't have to guess—*

Lloyd's voice was ragged. "Give me a chance to think about it. Please, Terry?"

She nodded reluctantly. She couldn't bear to see him hurt. Still.

"And please don't worry the children," Lloyd said. "Don't let them feel that we've been arguing—and especially not about them."

Terry said bitterly, "Always the psychologist!"

"Perhaps it was the father speaking that time." Lloyd turned and went up the ladder quickly. The port came open at his touch, swinging upward. The sound of laughter came through clearly now and childish voices shouting, "Daddy! Daddy! Look at me!"

Terry blinked fast to keep back the tears. "Lloyd! Lloyd!" she said. "If you only loved me!"

But she said it to herself.

They were sturdy boys, all brown long arms and legs and the kind of dark-brown eyes that seem almost black and look down deep inside a man. They floated in the center of the spherical recreation room, their faces laughing, their bodies as graceful as porpoises in the sea.

Lloyd looked at them and his heart grew cold. What would he be without them? An old man, dying.

"Hello, kids," he said. "What is it today?"

Paul answered. "We're playing Martians. He's the Martian. I'm an Earthman, and I try to catch him, because he's trying to keep me from getting to Mars. If I catch him in five jumps, I get to Mars, and if he gets away, I'm dead."

Carl chanted, "Nyah, nyah! You can't catch me!" He stuck out his tongue at Paul and pushed himself away. He hit the opposite wall and bounced back. In the middle, where there was no-gravity, he did a curious kind of flip that seemed to alter his direction. It must have been illusion. There was nothing for him to act against.

Lloyd had never seen anything like it.

Paul's hands, outstretched to catch his brother, missed by inches, and the older boy landed on the curved wall, his legs under him, bent and thrusting.

Lloyd jumped for the ceiling. Beside these brown, silken creatures he felt old and stiff. He touched the inner airlock door and slowly drifted from a handstand to his feet as the door opened. He slipped through.

He kept remembering their voices as he zipped himself with the ease of long practice into his suit. Children played like that. In the midst of wars they were soldiers. In the midst of plagues they were doctors and nurses. In the midst of space . . .

The other suits hung like decapitated monsters on the walls of the rectangular shaft. Terry's suit hadn't been used for a long time. He would have to check it carefully. If she were going to leave—

No. He wouldn't think of that.

He unlocked the outer door and slid through until he caught the hook-on ring. The door clanged shut. Now he could see the cottage from the outside. His home.

It was a sphere, a miniature world thirty feet in diameter, which is not so small in terms of living area when all of it is usable space. The sphere spun rapidly to give the illusion of one-third gravity in the rooms nearest the surface, diminishing rapidly toward the axis near which he stood. The axis consisted of the airlock, an imaginary cylinder through the recreation room, and the cargo hold at the other end.

Around the cottage was space—the night was a sooty black scattered with more stars than seemed possible to someone reared inside Earth's curtain of air.

There to the right was the red brilliance of Mars, closer than any of the others he could see, but still very, very far. To the left was Earth, 1,075 miles away, dark now with the sun and the moon both on the other side. It was a huge, black disk, dotted here and there with the reddish spots of cities, blotting out the stars, beneath one moment, hanging like a gigantic weight above him the next.

A man could do that to his senses out here where there was no up or down; where the only directions were here and away. He could drive himself mad with illusions. What must those poor lost souls out there near Mars be suffering, so far from home that Earth seemed like only another star among millions? He looked at Mars again, but he couldn't possibly glimpse the *Santa Maria*. Even the best telescope on the Wheel couldn't pick it out now.

A few hundred feet away was the Wheel, a spinning inner tube crossed by a single spoke, gleaming white in the starlight, against the velvet night. Around the Wheel were the spheres of other cottages—nine of them. Somehow they made the Wheel seem more like home. They humanized it, made it less like a foothold in space and more like a colony of men and women who were there and intended to stay. He *couldn't* let that be broken up.

It was hard on a woman. Men can live on dreams, sometimes, but women need solidity. But men need women and children, and always, somehow, they had induced women to go with them to the frontiers and build homes.

The question was: Had men gone so far that their women couldn't follow?

He launched himself toward the Wheel and floated effortlessly toward it. As he passed the round Hub at the center, he reached out with the hook of one sleeve-ending and caught the cage into which the taxis slipped with their human cargoes.

He went through the airlock, removed his suit and hung it on its rack, and clambered down the sagging netting to the weight control room. The air was bad in here—thick and hot and humid and filled with the many odors men make living and working. It was worse than the cottage.

Colonel Danton was waiting for him outside Celestial Observation. He looked old and haggard and sick. His hair was a thin, pure-white stubble on his head. His eyes were almost blind with cataracts, and his body was bent and thin. He looked eighty years old instead of less than fifty.

Phillips thought, *He won't be able to stand another failure.*

Danton said, "Jim Faust is here." His voice still carried the firmness and force of authority.

Lloyd said, "Here? What does he want?"

"He's worried. He wants to go over the tapes himself. He doesn't think he can carry us much longer—not if this shot fails."

Lloyd stared thoughtfully at Danton. "You don't need to go through this again. Take it easy this morning."

Danton's jaw tightened and then slowly relaxed. "Doctor's orders? Keep him happy, Lloyd. I'll see you at lunch."

Lloyd turned, opened the airtight door, and went into the darkness of the improvised viewing rooms where Faust was watching tapes of the fifth day. . . .

II

Five days out. The *Santa Maria* was one million miles from Earth. The ship was a child's toy of spheres and cylinders and rocket engines flimsily bolted together with pieces from an Erector set. It was all white; it gleamed like porcelain in the relentless sunlight.

The top half of the central cylinder was cargo space for equipment that would be needed for the investigation of Mars. Above that was the personnel sphere, dotted with portholes and shutter-like temperature regulators. There were three decks: the supply deck, with its lockers for spacesuits and its cylindrical airlock; the living deck; and the control deck. At the top was the plastic bubble of the astrodome.

The ship tumbled slowly as it coasted along the seven-hundred-and-thirty-five-million-mile ellipse which would carry it into the orbit of Mars at the instant the red planet would reach that point. The rocket motors had roared for fifteen minutes; the rest of the two-hundred-and-sixty-day trip would be in utter, inescapable silence.

Inside the sphere, the predominant impression was bare utility: everything was painted metal, plastic, and rubber tile. Every wall of the ship and much of the nominal floors and ceilings were used for gauges, ducts, lockers, bunks, chairs, tanks, conduits. . . .

The control deck was a closed universe of grinning gauges and shifting spots of colored light, but the man on watch glanced at them only occasionally. He was staring through the astrodome, watching for the Earth as the ship's slow tumbling brought it past.

Like all the crew members, Burt Holloway was a short man. He was a slim five feet seven with thin, mobile hands, short, blond hair, and very blue eyes. He was not handsome. Men said he had a monkey face, with his weak mouth and receding chin, but women thought he needed mothering. He was barefooted. His only garment was a pair of shorts.

Four of the crew were on the living deck, which was reached from either of the other two by concentric holes in the separating partitions bisected by a painted aluminum fireman's pole. Fastened to one curving wall were bunks which could be folded back. The other side of the room belonged to the dining unit: a snack dispenser, a giant freezer which extended into the storage deck, a short-wave range, and a circular table.

Jack "Iron" Barr, five feet eight of bulging muscles and matted red hair, lay in his bunk, his belt snapped to rings on the framework. He had dark blue eyes and eyebrows that met in a straight line above his crooked nose. He was reading a letter written on pale-blue note paper. Occasionally he brought it close to his face and sniffed, his eyes closed, a slow smile stretching his wide mouth.

"Hey, now," he said huskily. "Listen to this: 'Lover, honey, baby—I'll never forget that night you showed me—' "

"The Big Dipper," Ted Craddock finished. He was sitting in the slings of the table, a plastic flask of orange juice in one tanned hand. He was the baby of the group at twenty-five, a beautiful, brown-skinned young man. His hazel eyes squinted into laugh lines at the corners. "That woman must drench her note paper with musk. Put it away, Iron. It's stinking up the place." He broke off in a brief spell of coughing.

Barr said irritably, "It's better than the other stinks we breathe all the time. I swear I never knew you guys were so smelly. And you, Ted, spraying the place with germs. Why don't you cover your mouth? Hey, now, listen to this one." He drew a folded square of pink paper from under the waistband of his shorts. "This was a blond little joy baby—"

Emil Jelinek said quietly, "Knock it off, Iron." He was thirtyish to the others' late twenties, a thin, angular man with sparse black hair and a small, rakish mustache. He was lying in the bunk next to Barr, his hands folded behind his head. "Women are more than two and a half years away. By the time you get back they'll have two kids apiece."

"Not these," Barr boasted. "They'll wait. That's what Ellen says here. She says she'll wait for five years if she has to, or ten. She says there's nobody like me."

Tony Migliardo laughed from the other side of the deck where he floated beside the snack dispenser. He was a good-looking, dark-skinned young man with liquid brown eyes and blue-black hair. "There are many men like you, Iron, and she will find them —reproductive organs with minor attachments for mobility."

"You dirty little—" Barr tried to spring out of his bunk, but the belt pulled him back.

Jelinek turned his head and stared hard at Barr. "Everybody be quiet for ten seconds! If we're like this in five days, what will we be doing in two hundred and sixty? Mig? Do you hear me?"

"I am very sorry, Iron," Migliardo apologized. "I should not have said that."

Barr relaxed. "Okay then."

"And, Iron," Jelinek added, "I think it would be best if you didn't enlighten us on the details of your amorous conquests. There are enough natural irritants."

Barr grumbled, "You guys are missing your chance for the kind of education you don't get in the Academy. Go ahead. Stay stupid."

Craddock began to cough.

Barr twisted to stare at him. "What about that? That could get old, too."

Jelinek said, "I'll see what I can do. Ted?" He opened the locker beside his head and pulled an ophthalmoscope down.

Craddock freed himself from the table slings and floated over beside Jelinek's bunk. He held himself there with one hand while Jelinek inspected his throat. "The lining is irritated, but that could be just from coughing." He reached into the locker for a small metal cylinder. He flicked a small lever on the side. Two smooth, blue pills popped into his hand. "A little penicillin won't hurt. Come back for another in six hours."

Barr said suddenly, "Hey, now, Emil. That ain't right what you said about five days."

Migliardo glanced at the repeater clock on the wall. "Five days, one hour, sixteen minutes, thirty-one seconds."

Barr muttered, "That clock must be wrong. It's more like a month."

Jelinek said, "It's synchronized with the crystal-stabilized chronometer on the control deck. There isn't a more accurate timekeeper anywhere."

Barr grumbled, "I wouldn't put it past Phillips to rig it slow. He's full of tricks like that. Then when we were halfway and about to go batty, he'd tell us the trip was almost over. He'd think that was cute."

"Now, Iron," Craddock said, floating back toward the dining table, "what's the use of starting something like that, even as a joke?"

"Who's joking? I *know* we been gone more than five days."

Craddock caught the table edge and slipped his feet through the slings. "There's no radio—how could he tell us?"

Barr said sarcastically, "What do you think that swivel-mounted, parabolic dish antenna is for?"

"That's for telemetering the sounding rockets when we get to Mars."

"So they told us." Barr sneered. "But why is it always pointed toward Earth?"

Craddock said violently, "How do I know? Maybe it's telemetering our gauges."

"Telemetering! With the power that thing pulls? Are you kidding?"

Migliardo swallowed the bite of candy bar he had been chewing. "There's no big drain."

Barr looked at him scornfully. "That's why you're assistant engineer on this tub instead of engineer. The drain doesn't show on the gauge. I wondered why the reactor wasn't delivering its rated capacity. That dish out there takes part of it, and the power bypasses the gauge. It's gimmicked."

"Now, Iron," Migliardo said peacefully, "why would they do anything like that?"

"Why would they seal up a wall of the control deck and place it out of bounds?" Barr demanded. He twisted to face Jelinek. "You know more than anybody else."

Jelinek said calmly, "We were told that there is a safety factor in addition to the safety factors in fuel and structural strength."

"Why didn't they tell us what it was?"

"As a psychologist I can tell you that a safety factor you know all about isn't really a safety factor at all. You start figuring it in with the rated capacity. This is something we can depend on to get us through if everything else fails. We're better off not knowing exactly what it is."

Migliardo said, "Like believing in God."

Jelinek nodded. "It's a matter of faith."

Barr's lips curled. "Nuts. I want to *know.* I'll leave God to those who need him. He doesn't show up on any of my gauges. Take my word for it, this business of a safety factor is just as phony. They didn't tell us what it was because there isn't any. That sealed wall is nothing. If we opened it up, we'd find it as empty as the Pope's promises."

Migliardo said intensely, "Barr—!"

Jelinek's mild voice cut through. "Mig! Keep your opinions to yourself, Iron, and keep your hands off that panel. If it's empty we're better off not knowing. The time business that started this is absurd, and you know it. We check it every day when we figure our position."

"Well, yeah," Barr conceded, "but—"

Something went *pingngng!* The echoes raced through the ship. The lights went out. Somebody screamed, "Meteor!" Voices shouted a confused cacophony of orders. Bodies blundered about.

Then Barr said stridently, "Shut up! Everybody! It didn't hit the sphere. Burt? You all right?"

"Okay," Holloway called from the control deck. "But we're on battery now. I'm trying to locate the hit."

"No need," Barr said. "It's up ahead—in the reactor or the wiring between."

Craddock began, his voice quavering, "If it's the reactor—"

"We're dead," Barr said bluntly. "The battery will only last a few hours, and then the air conditioning goes off." There was a scuffling sound. "I'll go out and check. Mig. Suit up and get ready to lend a hand."

And then even the sound was gone.

III

In the viewing room of the Little Wheel, the screen was dark. Lloyd flipped on the lights and looked at Faust. The dapper little man was turning, his iron-gray, immaculate head becoming a finely chiseled face. He was no more than five feet four, but everything about him was in proportion, from his well-shod feet to his controlled face.

His smooth forehead was wrinkled now, his blue eyes hard. "It's you, Lloyd," he said, too quickly, in his big, orator's voice. "Was that the end? Is that what you are keeping from me?"

"Calm down, Jim," Lloyd said. "We're not keeping anything from you. The meteor didn't hit the reactor. It clipped a lead, and the *Santa Maria* went on battery. There wasn't enough power to give us anything but voice, and even that was a drain the ship couldn't take for long. Barr located the hole and spliced the lead in twenty-five minutes."

Faust relaxed. "Thank God for Barr. The rest of them sounded like an uninstructed delegation."

"Barr is the man of action," Lloyd said. "When the unexpected demanded quick, accurate action, he took charge. That's why he was there."

"Then he earned his passage. Let's get back to it."

"We have two hundred and fifty-nine days of tapes twenty-four hours a day."

Faust frowned. "Can I trust you to make a selection for me?"

Lloyd stood up. To him the room seemed big. It was Celestial Observation, a room about twenty feet high by twenty feet wide. To Faust, though, the room must seem cramped, sticky, and stinking. Of course, after ten years a man can get used to these things, just as he can get so used to a wife that he would be only part of a man if she should leave.

He took a chair close to Faust and looked squarely into the

politician's eyes. "You'll have to, Jim. What's got into you? You're our public relations man. You've trusted us before. I think you're the politician now, Jim."

"I'm both. The Party has consistently thrown its weight behind spaceflight, starting with the first mad rush to reach the S.1.1 in time to save Rev McMillen. We've fought your battles for more than thirty years, Lloyd. I think we deserve a little trust."

Lloyd said softly, "You've got it, you and the Party, but let's not put everything down to disinterested benevolence. You've done very well out of it, politically and financially. The Party is the most powerful single political force on Earth, even though it does not have an absolute majority. And you're the biggest voice in the Party.

"You've also done well personally. Nothing shady, I realize, but your side of the bread has been very well buttered. And you had some of your own money in the Big Wheel. You've made your profit. Now you say you can't trust us."

"Trust," Faust said, "is a two-way street."

Lloyd said slowly, "What would it do to public confidence if the world knew that the crew of the *Santa Maria* were bickering before the ship had been out a week?"

"The stock market would take it hard."

Lloyd spread his hands expressively. "So?"

"So I'm here, Lloyd," Faust said evenly. "*I* have to know the truth. The planets aren't indispensable. We can relax for a few years, consolidate our gains, forget about Mars and Venus."

"What about the surpluses, Jim? What about the economic dislocation?"

"Better a dislocation now that we can ride than a crash later that will throw us all into the mud and put somebody like Deacon McIntire in the saddle. We can stand a dislocation if we handle it right, if we *prepare* the public for another failure. They've seen two ships sail right past Mars and sweep back. If we broke the news of this failure suddenly, there would be chaos—political and economic. McIntire would gain enough of our shocked voters to give his Fundamentalist Coalition a clear majority. Once he's in, we couldn't get him out. We'd have to assassinate him, and that would really tear it. I don't want to see that, Lloyd. Space is important, but it's not as important as people. We can come back, Lloyd, if we aren't torn apart now."

"There's a saying about fighters. They never come back. Everything has its psychological moment. This is it for Mars. It's now or never."

Faust's voice was regretful. "Maybe you're right. It may be never. If that happens I'll be very, very sorry. But I'll live, and so will you. I'd like to see Earth go on living, too, even without the stars."

Lloyd said in amazement, "You really are prepared to throw us over! The Party has been identified with spaceflight. Could you shake that tag?"

Faust hesitated. "It would be rough, but we could do it. Space has been good to us—all of us, not just the Party. The people would understand retrenchment. But they would have to be prepared for it. Starting now."

"Sure, Jim," Lloyd said bitterly. . . . "But you've got to understand. Everything isn't what it seems. It takes interpretation." He spoke briefly into the wall mike. "Here's the thirtieth day."

IV

Thirty days out. The *Santa Maria* was five and one-half million miles from Earth. The planet was still a perceptible disk, but the moon beside it had dwindled to a point. Both were still the most brilliant bodies in the universe, excepting the sun. Holloway stood at the dark port staring back the way they had come at the planet called home. He did not move; he scarcely seemed to blink.

The living deck of the personnel sphere was completely quiet. It was a silence which could not even be imagined by anyone except a spaceman. Then came a slap of a magnetized card on the dining table where Craddock and Migliardo were playing gin rummy.

Craddock coughed and laid his ten cards face down on the table while he covered his mouth with both hands. The paroxysm jarred him, shaking his whole body.

Migliardo picked up a flask and shoved it into Craddock's hand. Barr twisted in his bunk, a stereoscopic viewer held carelessly in one hand. He shouted, "Knock it off! Knock it off!"

Craddock squeezed water into his mouth, swallowed convulsively between coughs, and squeezed again until all the water was gone. Slowly the seizure eased. Craddock wiped tears from his eyes. "Thanks, Mig," he said weakly. He had grown thinner. They all had.

"Emil!" Barr shouted from his bunk "Why the hell don't you do something about that?"

Jelinek's calm voice floated to them from the control deck. "I've told you, Iron, it's psychosomatic."

Barr muttered, "If somebody doesn't do something, Ted is gonna wake up some morning without a throat to cough through."

Jelinek's thin face appeared in the hole. "What do you mean by that, Iron?"

"Just what I said."

Craddock said apologetically, "He didn't mean anything. It gets on his nerves, my coughing all the time. Hell, it gets on my nerves, too."

Jelinek hadn't moved. "We're all in this together, Iron. We all get through or none of us. Oh, I know—maybe Mig could take over for you and do a job that might be good enough. Burt could pilot the ship if something happened to me. Mig could navigate for Burt if he had to, and you know enough about wiring and electronics to do the essentials of Ted's work. But actually it wouldn't work out that way. There's five of us. That's a bare minimum for sanity. Any less and none of us would make it."

His face disappeared and silence descended again. Barr shrugged and looked back into his stereoscopic viewer. Craddock and Migliardo drew cards from the thick pack on the table and slapped them down. Holloway stared silently out the port.

Jelinek said, "Tank B is starting to freeze. I'm going to rotate it into sunlight."

Nobody moved or looked up. Somewhere in the ship a motor whined as it accelerated a flywheel. Very slowly the ship began to turn. The whine descended the scale again, faded into silence.

Holloway screamed. He pointed a shaking finger at the port as everyone turned toward him and Jelinek's face appeared in the opening.

"What the—!"

"Burt!"

"For God's sake, Burt!"

"There—" Holloway said. "There was something—out there!"

"What was it?" Jelinek said. "Try to tell us what you saw."

Holloway clung to a handhold by the port and shook. His body floated out in the air. "I don't know what it was. Something—something white. It's gone now."

Jelinek said sharply, "You saw more than that to make you scream. What was it, Burt?"

Migliardo said softly, "It could be garbage, perhaps."

"Yes," Holloway said quickly. "That was it. Floating beside the ship. When you turned the ship, it went past the port."

Jelinek said insistently, "Maybe that was it, Burt, but what did you think it was?"

Angrily Holloway said, "All right! It looked like a face, a face with a beard!"

"Look like anybody you ever saw?" Jelinek asked.

Holloway's shaking had dropped to occasional tremors. "I'm not crazy, Emil. No, I never saw that face before."

"Did it look dead?"

"No!"

"How do you know?"

Holloway took a deep breath and said steadily, "It looked in at me. It saw me. Its eyes—I never saw such a look of sorrow and pity before. It felt—sorry for me. Sorry for all of us."

"For God's sake!" Barr complained. "I never heard so much bull in my life. You'd just been burning your eyes out looking at Earth and the moon. It was an after-image."

Jelinek nodded. "I suppose that was it—superimposed upon a flash of sunlight. Or maybe, like Mig said, some trash. Don't let it worry you, Burt."

Holloway laughed shakily. "Who's worrying? What could be out here, almost six million miles from anywhere?"

"Hey, now," Barr said. "Here's something worth looking at." He flipped the plastic viewer toward Holloway.

Holloway caught it, put it up to his eyes, and stared into it. "So that's what you've been having such a time with!" he said flatly.

Craddock said eagerly, "Let me see!"

Holloway tossed it to him as if he were getting rid of filth. Then he wiped his hand on his shorts and turned back to the port.

Craddock stared into the viewer for a long time, clicked another scene into place, and stared again. His cheeks grew flushed.

Migliardo was watching him curiously. "What's this all about?" He reached over to grab the viewer.

"You'll get your turn!" Craddock said.

Migliardo yanked it away. "You can have it back." He stared into it and then hastily tore it away from his eyes. "In the name of—" He crossed himself automatically. "How did you you smuggle these damned things aboard? Can't you find anything better to do than staring at these dirty—?"

Craddock held out his hand. "Give it back! Give it to me!"

Jelinek's head was looking through the hole again. "I swear I spend more time looking at you idiots than I do looking at the gauges. Let me see that!"

Migliardo flicked it contemptuously toward Jelinek. He reached for it, but the viewer sailed through the hole and out of sight. A moment later there was a crash of plastic against metal.

Barr released his belt hooks in a swift, practiced movement and sprang toward the pole. He stared through the hole at Jelinek, who appeared again holding the smashed viewer.

"Sorry, Iron," Jelinek said apologetically. "Clumsy of me."

Barr said furiously, "If I thought you did that on purpose—"

"You'd what?" Jelinek asked calmly.

In a cold, deadly voice Barr said, "I'd beat you until you'd walk out that airlock without a suit rather than stay in here with me. It's ruined," he wailed.

"I'm not really sorry," Jelinek said. "Can't you understand that dirty pictures just aren't the proper thing for a two-and-a-half year stag cruise. The only way you'll get back to women is by *not* thinking about them."

Barr said angrily, "Give it to me!" He grabbed the wreckage from Jelinek's hand. "You get by your way, and I'll get by mine." His eyes held a heavy-lidded look of dislike. "Don't get in my way again, headshrinker, or one of us won't get back."

Barr slipped his thick, hairy legs into two table straps and carefully put the smashed viewer on the table. None of the pieces were missing. Carefully, with a great delicacy in his thick fingers, he separated the broken segments and gently placed them on the table. "Hey, Burt," he called, "throw me that tube of liquid cement in my locker."

In a moment it came sailing toward him. Barr raised a careless hand and plucked it out of the air. The movement stirred the pieces on the table, and Barr covered them quickly to keep them from blowing away. Slowly, moistening each edge with clear cement he began to fit the pieces together.

Migliardo went "gin," and he gleefully added up the score.

Holloway stared out the port, unmoving.

"I'm hungry," Barr said suddenly. "You're cook today, Mig. Put something on. I'd go for a nice, juicy steak today."

"We had steak yesterday," Migliardo said absently, studying his cards.

"I don't care when we had steak," Barr said. "I want steak today."

"If we eat steak once a week, we have enough to last for the whole trip," Migliardo said. "If we eat it every day, we will have none for two years. Today we will have filet of sole."

"What is this—Friday?" Barr asked.

"As a matter of fact," Migliardo said, "it is."

Barr sneered. "You fish eaters don't have to eat fish any more, haven't you heard? And I hate fish!"

"There is fish enough for fish once a week," Migliardo said calmly. "Friday is as good a day as any other. You liked fish before."

Barr slammed his hand down on the table. "Well, now I hate it! I tell you what," he said slyly, "you eat my fish and I'll eat your steak."

"No, thank you," Migliardo said politely. "I like fish once a week. I like steak once a week, too. Anyhow—" Migliardo glanced up at the clock—"it is not time for supper."

Barr roared, "That clock's wrong! Which are you gonna believe, my stomach or that clock? I know which I'm gonna believe." He slipped his legs out of the slings and pulled himself around to the deep freeze beside the range. He sorted through the prepared meals until he found what he wanted and slipped it into the range.

Migliardo started to say something, shrugged, and closed his mouth. Craddock threw down a card.

"Gin!" Migliardo said triumphantly, putting down his cards. "That's three hundred and twelve dollars you owe me."

Craddock stared down incredulous. Suddenly he looked up and threw his cards into Migliardo's face. "Cheater!" he shouted hysterically. "You lousy cardsharp, I'm not going to pay you! I'm not going to play any more, either! You're a dirty dago cardsharp!"

He broke off in a convulsion of coughs that racked his body and made his hazel eyes bulge in their sockets. Migliardo stared at him in astonishment, blood oozing from a cut under his left eye where the corner of one card had hit him.

The screen went dark.

V

As the lights came on, Faust turned quickly toward Lloyd. "Another meteor?"

"End of the reel."

Faust's breath sighed out. "It doesn't look good."

Lloyd said, "Don't be misled. We're showing the worst of it. There are many days when life went on in an ordinary, uneventful fashion. No arguments, no fights, no disagreements."

"Something like that once a month would be too often. . . . It seems like—an oddly assorted group of men that was chosen."

Lloyd smiled. "Criticism intended? We picked them carefully, first looking for crew balance, then the necessary skills. They were intended to complement each other, one man's weakness against another's strength. We tried to figure pressures, the abrasion of personalities, the pecking order—but it's like trying to predict the nature of matter on Jupiter. Those men are living out there under conditions about which we had no information—when we chose them. We're getting it now."

Faust looked curiously at Lloyd. "I thought those men were friends of yours."

Lloyd's face hardened. "They are. Every one of them. You

wouldn't put a friend through a test to destruction? Maybe not. But you'd nominate the best candidate and then watch his campaign closely, so that if he fails you won't make the same mistake again. I don't want to send out any more men blind."

Faust frowned. "I see. But doesn't the video equipment take up space that could be used for something that could help them survive? More food and water? Enough steak so that Barr could have one every day? Radio receiving equipment?"

Lloyd shook his head. "If there were enough steaks, Barr wouldn't be interested. His drive is psychological—all their drives are. Receiving equipment isn't a help but a threat to their sanity. How would you feel if you knew you were cut off, irretrievably, from the rest of humanity for a minimum of two and a half years, and you could hear, constantly, the reminder that men were living safe, sane, happy lives, that they were eating anything they wanted, going to ball games, sleeping with women, walking out on the green Earth? It would drive you mad.

"We tried that on the *Pinta* and the *Niña*. On the *Pinta* the radio was smashed the first week. On the *Niña* it lasted ten days. Those men are cut off. They must know it, know that they can receive no help, that they're on their own. Psychologically they must feel that life has stopped for everyone else, too. If they can get back, they will find everything just as it was when they left, the same friends, the same jobs, the same girls to love them. No, receiving equipment isn't the answer."

Faust said, "You sound as if you're trying to convince yourself."

"You think I'm not? You think I don't dread watching these tapes? And yet I look forward to it with a fascination that horrifies me.

"And still I know that those men have enough to get them through—if men can get through at all. They have more than enough food, more than enough fuel, more than enough air. And on top of that, there is a safety factor."

Faust's eyes brightened. "Ah, the mysterious safety factor. I had almost forgotten that. What is it?"

Lloyd hesitated. "I'd rather you saw for yourself. It worked out rather—oddly." He glanced at his wrist watch. "How about lunch? Amos is waiting."

Faust's voice mellowed. "Amos looks worse than a year ago. How long is he going to last?"

"Not long enough to do what he wants to do."

"Why hasn't he ever made general?"

"He's turned it down repeatedly. A colonel commands the Little Wheel. Inside, they think it's not a big enough job for a general. Take his job away and he'd die. Physiologically it would be disastrous. Don't tell him I told you—he's got a bad heart. Heavy primary damage. He'll live longer here."

"You've never made general yourself," Faust said. "How many promotions have you turned down?"

"A few," Lloyd said curtly. "Here we are." He pulled open a door, and they were in the mess hall, three long aluminum tables with benches attached. The room was empty except for Amos Danton, who sat next to the delivery chute of the electronic range. He was staring expressionlessly at his tray as the door opened, but he looked up, smiling, as they entered.

"I've taken the liberty of ordering for you," he said.

They seated themselves at the trays and set to work. Danton, Lloyd noticed, had only a chef's salad. He stirred it around with his fork, but Lloyd did not see him take a bite.

He loved this man, this carved, blackened face with the almost-blind eyes and the thin stubble of white hair, this hard, talented leader of men who had sent too many of them to their deaths and had died with every one of them, this strange, dedicated space-farer, this father-image.

Danton was saying quietly, "What do you think, Jim? You know men, and you're fresh. You haven't lived with it as we have. Is it bad?"

Faust nodded slowly. "It will be a miracle if they make it."

Danton groaned. "And you've only seen the first thirty days. Lloyd, I told you I should have gone. You should have let me go."

Lloyd started to speak, but Faust was there ahead of him. "No, Amos. You were indispensable. Without you there would be nothing here now. You're still indispensable."

"I'd like to believe you," Danton said, covering his face with a wrinkled hand. "But Lloyd can carry on." He turned fiercely on Lloyd. "You *will* carry on, Lloyd! You can't have any life but this." He looked toward the open port, where the many-colored stars turned endlessly. "The old order passeth. The day of the unspecialized spaceman is done. Now comes the psychologist who can fit men to space and not space to men."

Lloyd said, "Ready?"

Danton rose with them.

Lloyd turned to Faust. "Go on ahead, will you, Jim?"

Faust nodded and headed briskly for the door.

When they were alone, Lloyd said, "Amos, Terry is leaving me."

Danton closed his eyes for a moment and then looked with concern at Lloyd. "Taking the kids?"

"So she says. She's had it, Amos. I've seen it coming for years. I've tried to stave it off, but what can you do when a woman wants the company of sane people with their feet on the ground, wants her children to run across green lawns bareheaded in the sunshine, to play baseball and football, go to dances and sit with a girl under a full moon? How can you argue with that?"

"You don't argue, son. Even a man who's never had a wife can tell you that much."

"I've thought of one thing," Lloyd said slowly. "We went wrong when we built the cottages. There's too much loneliness out here already without adding more. We've got nine families and one empty cottage since Chapman's wife left him. Let's connect the nine together with the empty one in the middle. That one we'll convert into a recreation center with lounges, a dance floor, card rooms, a gym in the center. The women can get together without going outside, and the crewmen can use it, too. Can we afford it?"

Danton nodded. "Sounds like mostly labor, and we've got nothing to work on, now. We not only can afford it, we can't afford not to have it. But that isn't going to solve your problem."

Lloyd's face turned gloomy again. "I know."

"I hate to sound like an advice-to-the-lovelornist," Danton said, "but women need security. Emotional security. How long has it been since you showed Terry that you love her?"

"Too long," Lloyd said soberly. And then with a sudden explosion of better spirits, he said, "Let's go see the tapes."

VI

Seventy-three days out. The ungainly contraption of fuel tanks and rocket motors and fragile living space, the *Santa Maria*, was twelve million miles from Earth. For the last few days, the bright double star that was the Earth and the moon had slowly dimmed and disappeared. It had turned its night side to the ship.

This time the ship was not quiet. Music pounded throughout the personnel sphere, with wild riffs, the sudden brassy blare of trumpets, the low dirty growling of slide trombones. Holloway was on watch. He was staring through the combination telescope and celestial camera at the spectacular event that was about to begin.

Craddock was at the water spigot, filling his flask. Coughs occasionally shook his body. His face looked quite thin now; he seemed years older.

Barr was lying in his bunk. He was reading a paperback book. Occasionally a chuckle broke through the crash of the music.

Jelinek and Migliardo clung to the handholds at the port. A

thick, translucent shield had been slipped over it, but the sun was still a white-hot disk through it.

"Iron!" Craddock said suddenly, "can't you turn down that noise just a little? We've heard those tapes twenty times."

Barr said, "It's better than listening to you hack all the time."

Jelinek said, not looking around, "Just a little lower, Barr. That's not asking much."

"The hell it isn't," Barr said.

"Mig?" Jelinek asked. "Too loud?"

"Too loud," Mig said.

"Three of us say it's too loud, Iron. We don't need to bother Burt. You're outvoted. Turn it down."

"Screw you!" Barr said.

Jelinek spun to Barr's bunk and twisted the knob on the stanchion. The music stopped. Instantly Barr had Jelinek's thin wrist in his big left hand. The bones grated together. Barr pulled himself up to Jelinek's face in the silence that was more absolute than the grave.

Barr said, "I like it, see! The silence is too loud; you have to drown it out. I want life around me, if I have to kill every one of you. Now leave me alone!" He threw Jelinek's arm away, switched the music to its highest volume, and let the straps pull him back into a floating position above his bunk.

Jelinek looked down at his wrist. White fingermarks ate deep into the tanned skin. Slowly they turned red. He chewed at the end of his mustache. It had grown ragged. Then he turned, shrugging, and caught the handhold by the port. Migliardo looked at him questioningly. Jelinek lifted an eyebrow helplessly.

Barr roared, "And get away from that water, Craddock!"

Craddock jumped. He said sullenly, "There's lots of water."

"Not the way you've been lapping it up," Barr said. "Every time I look I see you sneaking another drink."

"I'm allotted four and a half pounds a day. And you know it."

"You've been swilling twice that. Cut it out, or I'll have to put a lock on it like I put on the freezer to keep you guys out of the steaks."

Jelinek said, "There's more than enough water, Barr. If we get desperate, we've got utility water."

Barr looked at Jelinek, his lip curling contemptuously. "Would you drink that stuff?"

"Yes."

"I guess you would! Well, I won't. I want clean water. Lots of it. You want to make it hard on yourself, go ahead!"

Jelinek said carefully, "Don't drive us too hard, Barr. We'll let you have the steaks, we'll let you—"

"Who's letting me?" Barr said brutally. "I'm taking!"

"We'll let you drive us a ways, because we're all on the *Outward Bound* together. But if you push us too far, we may decide that we have a better chance without you."

"Screw you! You mother-fucking bastards wouldn't crock a flea if it was crawling on your—"

Mig shouted, "Emil! It's starting!"

Jelinek swung around. Across the flaming disk of the sun edged a small black spot. It was Earth. They were seeing what few other eyes had ever seen—a transit of the Earth and moon. An hour later a smaller speck would appear and follow the Earth toward the sun's blazing center. The transit would last eight hours.

Holloway called exultantly, "Thirteen hundred twelve and six seconds. Right on the nose."

Migliardo said, "I'd better give Burt a hand. We need these readings for course correction." He swung to the pole and pulled himself toward the control deck.

Craddock looked at Barr and said, "I'm going to check on the supplies." He coughed and disappeared through the hole leading to the storage deck.

When they were alone, Jelinek said to Barr, "Turn it down a little, Barr. I want to talk to you, and I'd rather the others didn't hear. It isn't often any two of us are alone."

Sullenly Barr reached over and switched the music down.

Jelinek moved his hand impatiently. "What are you trying to do, Barr?"

"Get what's mine."

"All the steaks? That's yours? Listen, Barr!" Jelinek said urgently. "We could be just as hard as you are. But we know we're living in an egg shell. We're all together on the *Outward Bound*—"

"It's the *Santa Maria*," Barr snapped.

"Sorry. Bad habit. What I'm trying to say is—we know that our lives depend on you. In the same sense, your life depends on every one of us. You can't get back without me, Barr. I'm the pilot. If something happens to me, you're dead. Get that! Dead, dead, dead! No more steaks, then, Barr. No more women. No more Barr."

"I don't scare worth a damn, Jelinek."

"Barr! It's time you were scared. We're looking death right in the face. If you aren't scared now, there's no help for any of us!"

"Shut up!" Barr screamed. "Shut up or I'll shut you up! We're in no more danger than we were on that joy ride to the moon. We've got it made, Emil! We're only ten days out."

"Barr. This is only the seventy-third day. We've got one hundred and eighty-seven to go."

"You're trying to scare me," Barr said quickly. "I've kept track. Don't look at the clock! It's wrong. They're trying to trick us, Phillips is. I know how he works. We're almost there, Emil. Don't lie to me! It's true, isn't it? We're almost—"

Jelinek was shaking his head slowly. "It would be no kindness to let you go on thinking that. Look out there—a transit of the Earth and moon. Seventy-three days out, Barr, exactly."

Barr's eyes were bulging with fear; his chest drew in huge gulps of air. "No, no. . . ."

Craddock's voice floated up gleefully from the storage deck. "Barr, I just urinated in the water supply. Hear me, Barr? What will you drink now, Barr?"

Anger contorted Barr's face like an expression of relief. He started up. "That filthy, little—"

Jelinek shoved him back. "He's lying, Barr. There's no way to get into the water supply down there. But that's how far you've driven him."

Barr's eyes gleamed savagely. "He'd find a way. He hates me. You all hate me. I don't give a damn! You all watch me and talk about me and plot against me! Go ahead. I can take you one at a time or all at once."

There was a scrambling sound as Craddock went through the airlock door, and a clang as it slammed down. Barr said viciously, "I'll get the little bastard when he comes back in."

"This morning when I came on watch," Jelinek said slowly, "I found tool marks around the sealed panel on the control deck. They weren't there yesterday. You had the watch before mine."

Barr sneered. "So what?"

"You've been trying to get in there. You're going to stop, Barr. If I find any more tool marks around that panel, I'm going to kill you, Barr. It would be easy for me. A hypodermic some night, a little arsenic on one of the steaks. You stay away from that panel!"

After a moment Barr said, "You wouldn't dare kill me. You're too careful. It would reduce your chances of getting through."

"I wouldn't take a chance on it if I were you, Barr," Jelinek said.

The music clicked back up. The beat made the ship vibrate.

There was a scrambling sound from the supply deck. Jelinek turned. Craddock, in full spacesuit, was drifting along the pole. Through the faceplate Jelinek could see Craddock's face contorted, his eyes staring, his mouth open.

Jelinek sprang toward him and started loosening the wing nuts that held the helmet in place. He pulled the helmet off. Craddock's screams rose above the crash of the music. They came out one after another with scarcely time between for a breath.

"Ted!" Jelinek shouted. He slapped him across the face,

clutching one arm of Craddock's suit to keep from being spun across the room.

Craddock's screams stopped suddenly. The room was horribly silent.

Craddock drew a shuddering breath, closed his eyes, and opened them. Sanity had come back into them.

Jelinek said forcefully, "What happened, Ted?"

"I was—going down—to check—on the supplies—" He drew in another ragged breath. "I saw him. Somebody back there. He came out from behind one of the sounding missiles."

"What did he look like?"

"Pale face. Beard. Very white hands—"

Jelinek said sharply, "How could you see his hands if he had on a suit?"

"No suit. He had a sort of cloth around his hips like a sloppy pair of shorts. No helmet, no suit."

Somebody said, "Stowaway!"

Jelinek looked toward the hole leading to the control deck. Two faces were framed there: Migliardo's, dark and frowning; Holloway's, white, stricken. Holloway had spoken.

"There's no air back there," Jelinek said. "No food or water. No way a man could live for five minutes, much less seventy-three days."

Holloway said, "It doesn't have to be a man."

Barr shouted, "What else could it be?"

Holloway didn't say anything.

Barr shouted, "What are you trying to do, scare me? It's just a joke, eh, Ted? Trying to get even?"

"No joke to him, Barr," Jelinek said. "He's terrified. It was an illusion. We're all liable to see things. It's when we all see the same thing that it will be too late. Barr, go down and see what it was."

Barr swung himself out of his bunk eagerly. "You bet."

Jelinek snapped. "Mig! Help me get this suit off."

Craddock couldn't seem to move at all. After the suit was removed, he trembled in every muscle. Every few seconds he would cough. Migliardo guided him toward his bunk. As Migliardo strapped him down, Jelinek got a hypodermic from his locker.

"I'll give him some reserpine."

Migliardo said softly, "Did Ted's description remind you of anything?"

"The face Burt saw through the port. It's natural. Suggestion is a powerful force."

Another scream came from the storage deck. Jelinek and Migliardo stiffened, but this was a scream of rage. Barr swarmed into the room along the pole. He hung there like an angry, red moneky. "Somebody tried to kill me!"

"We were all here," Jelinek said.

Barr's voice rose higher. "Somebody's been messing with the oxygen gauge on my suit. The gauge reads full, but the tank is empty."

"It must have been an accident," Jelinek said briskly.

"I know who did it," Barr shouted. "That little sneak lying there." He pointed a trembling finger at Craddock. "He did it before he said he ruined the water. He wanted me to chase him outside. Then he'd come back and you'd say it was an accident. Too bad."

"That's absurd, Barr!" Jelinek snapped. "Clip on another tank and check around the sounding missiles!"

Barr swung toward him viciously. "Unh-unh! Maybe something else is wrong with the suit. It'd be easy to poke a pinhole in one of the joints, jigger a valve. . . . I'm never gonna use that suit. If you want to kill me, you'll have to do it where I can see you." He was shaking all over.

Jelinek said, "Mig. Go check."

Mig swung along the pole.

"Barr!" Jelinek said. "Lie down. Read one of your filthy books.

Just shut up!'' He looked toward Holloway's white face and staring blue eyes. "Burt! Get back on watch!''

An unnatural silence fell over the sphere.

Minutes passed. No one moved. Finally there was the clang of the airlock door and then the sounds of someone stripping off his suit.

"Nothing," Migliardo said, coming along the pole. "Nothing white. Nothing moving. Nothing.''

Beyond the port, the transit of the Earth and moon was proceeding placidly.

VII

Jim Faust was shaking his head as Lloyd turned on the lights. His face was as pale as Holloway's had been. "Bad," he muttered. "Bad, real bad.''

"Remember," Lloyd said, "that you're seeing the worst of them. They aren't all like that.''

"God," Faust muttered, "how I hate that Barr!''

Lloyd cleared his throat. "He's a good man. He was our extrovert. Balance. If they'd all been like Migliardo or Jelinek, they'd all be insane by now, drawn into fetal positions. Barr gives them something to hate. We didn't figure it that way, but it happened.''

Faust said, "You can't live with hate.''

"Sometimes," Lloyd said, "you can't live without it. The *Santa Maria* has been operational for almost five times as long as the *Pinta*, for three times as long as the *Niña.''*

"Better isn't good enough," Faust said.

"In some of the reels we skipped," Lloyd said, "Jelinek had started psychoanalysis.''

Faust said bluntly, "He's not qualified to give it. The man's not sane himself. He can't control Barr. He's already threatened him with death. That's not the act of a sane psychologist. Barr's fright-

ened enough as it is. He has tried to convince himself that the trip
is almost over. But he knows this isn't true, and he compensates
by acting the petty tyrant. You can't frighten a man who's already
scared to death."

"Jelinek has pinned his faith on that sealed panel," Lloyd said.
"Barr threatens that faith. What about Migliardo?"

"Compared to the others, he seems sane. Maybe he's just
quiet. He's probably going quietly mad inside. They all have
symptoms of paranoia. People are plotting against them, spying
on them—"

Lloyd shook his head. "Let's watch the next reel."

Faust and Danton turned their swivel chairs toward the frosted
screen as Lloyd flipped off the lights.

VIII

One hundred and thirty-three days out. The *Santa Maria*
coasted silently along the seven-hundred-and-thirty-five-million-
mile ellipse that would bring it finally to Mars. Inside the personnel sphere it was silent, too.

The ports were all closed. The room was dark. It was 0300 by
ship's time. It was part of the enforced period of inactivity the
crew called night in a place where the sun never set, where the
night was all about them eternally.

Only the deep, regular breathing of men at sleep could be
heard and occasionally a relay clicking on the control deck. Then
a dark figure twisted in its bunk and started screaming.

Men tumbled out of their bunks, scrambling in the weightlessness for a handhold.

Migliardo found the light switch, and the room sprang into
prosaic reality from its shadowed horror. Jelinek, Barr, and Migliardo were floating in the air. Holloway had pushed himself up
in his bunk. He was still screaming.

Jelinek wrapped his thin legs around a stanchion and shook Holloway violently. The navigator's eyes opened blankly as his head flopped. He saw Jelinek. He stopped screaming.

"What the hell happened to you?" Barr asked querulously.

"I had a dream," Holloway said. "I dreamed I was falling."

"Oh, for God's sake!" Barr said with great disgust. "One of those. I wish I had a cigarette. I'd give my right nut for a cigarette."

Holloway went on as if he hadn't heard. His eyes were distant and remembering. "I dreamed I was dead. I was in a metal coffin, and I was falling. I would never be buried, and so I could never rest. I was dead, but I could still hear and see and feel, and I could never rest because I was in a metal coffin, and I was falling."

Migliardo said quietly, "Aren't we all?"

Barr twisted around fiercely. "Aren't we all *what?*"

Jelinek said. "We're all in a metal coffin, and we call it the *Outward Bound.*"

Migliardo looked at him. "I finally remembered where I heard that name. It was an old play. A group of people were on this ship, heading for an unknown port. And they finally realized they were all dead."

Jelinek said ruefully, "A man's subconscious plays tricks on him."

Barr had been glancing back and forth between them, a look of horror growing on his face. "What are you guys talking about? We aren't dead."

"No," Jelinek said. "It's a grisly joke, and one we can't afford."

"Emil," Holloway said in a quiet and terrible voice. "Emil. Ted's lying there in his bunk. He hasn't moved."

Ted's bunk was next to Holloway's. Jelinek spun around the end of it and caught the aluminum framework. He stared down at Craddock. "Mig. Throw me my stethoscope." But he didn't wait for it; he put his ear to Craddock's chest. In a moment he let his head float upright. "Never mind," he said softly. "He's dead."

Migliardo crossed himself and began murmuring something under his breath. Barr's eyes bulged with terror. Holloway floated over his bunk, shaking, hugging himself.

"I'm cold," Holloway said vaguely. "Don't you think it's cold in here? The air is bad, too. I think I'm going to be sick."

Jelinek began an inspection of Craddock's body. Suddenly he looked up sharply and glanced around the room as if he were counting them. His lips moved. "Who's on watch?" he asked sharply. "Barr. This is your trick, isn't it?"

"Shepherd offered to take it," Barr said sullenly.

"He's been standing a lot of your watches, hasn't he?"

"No more than for Burt or Ted." Barr's voice was shaky. "What killed him?"

"Not what," Jelinek said slowly. "Who. Ted was murdered."

In the silence, Jelinek looked at each of them.

"How do you know?" Barr said. "He was dying. We all knew that. He hasn't been able to keep down any food for a month."

"Somebody couldn't wait. He was strangled."

"W-who—" Holloway stammered, "who—who did it?"

Jelinek looked at each of them soberly. "Do we really want to know? If we know, we'll have to do something about it. If we aren't sure, then we can go on pretending."

"And leave a murderer unmarked among us?" Migliardo said. "How can we be sure he won't kill again?" He looked from Barr to Holloway to Jelinek.

Barr said, "Maybe the murderer doesn't even know it. Anybody who'd do a thing like that would have to be cracked. He—he wouldn't necessarily know he had done it."

"That's a good point," Jelinek said. "Maybe we have a homicidal schizo among us. I think you're right, Mig. We should know. So we can tell the murderer who he is."

"How can you be sure?" Holloway said weakly. "Anybody could have done it. Barr—you were always fighting with him about his coughing and drinking. You said you'd kill him. Now you've done it! Just as you said!"

"Me!" Barr said, outrage in his voice. "What about you? You hated him. You wanted to trade bunks with Mig so you wouldn't have to sleep next to him. Or Mig! You fought with him, too, Mig. He called you a dirty, dago cardsharp. . . ."

Jelinek said wearily, "Who didn't fight with him—and with everybody else? Anyway, Ted marked the murderer for us. He was stronger than the murderer thought. He's got skin under his fingernails. A little blood, too. It belongs to the murderer. And the murderer has marks on his arms where Ted clawed him in the final struggle. Everybody hold out their arms."

Holloway was staring at his already; so was Migliardo. Holloway held his arms out eagerly. "No scratches. See? Nothing."

"Mig?"

With an expression of relief, Mig held his arms out.

"You're clean. Iron?"

Barr put his arms behind him. "Let's see yours."

Jelinek held out his arms and turned them over slowly so that the palms were down. They were unmarked. "Iron?"

Barr hesitated. "I scratched my arms yesterday trying on my suit. Somebody has been messing with it again. Somebody's been trying to kill *me!* That's the one to look for." The words came spilling from his mouth. "He couldn't get me so he got Ted. Ted was easy. Ted was dying anyway. I'm too tough, so he got Ted. Somebody's been watching us, trying to kill us, and he finally saw his chance."

"Iron?" Jelinek repeated quietly.

"What about Shepherd?" Barr asked eagerly. "Why don't you look at his arms?"

"I don't think we have to look any farther. Anybody who won't show his arms must be sure he's guilty."

Barr said suddenly, "It's a trick. I bet there isn't any skin under Ted's fingernails. You just said that because you saw my arms yesterday when I scratched them." He pushed himself toward Ted's bunk. "You're trying to trick me into saying I killed him."

"Look!" Migliardo said and pointed at Barr's arm.

On the outside of the arm, just above the wrist, were three long, red, vertical scratches. Serum oozed from them.

Barr hid the arm in front of him. "I didn't kill him!" he shouted hysterically. "I'd remember if I killed him. I don't remember." His voice trailed away in hysterical sobs.

"What now?" Migliardo asked.

Jelinek's eyebrows lifted. "I suppose we might as well have the funeral."

Holloway said, "What are you going to do with the body?"

Jelinek said, "Give it a spaceman's burial. It's all we can do."

"And have him follow the ship to Mars?" Holloway's voice quavered. "See him floating out there every time we look out?"

"If we give it a good shove," Jelinek said, "it would be out of sight in a few hours."

"He should be buried," Holloway muttered. "He won't stay quiet unless he's buried."

Jelinek shrugged. "We'll give him a spaceman's burial—he'd have wanted that. Do you know any of the ceremony, Mig?"

"I'll try."

"Food," Barr said craftily. "We may run short of food. What's the use of throwing away—"

"If we ever get that desperate," Jelinek said sadly, "we'll be finished. Unfasten him from the bunk. Bring him to the storage deck."

Barr shoved himself away from the bunk. "Me? I don't want to touch him. Somebody else. I can't do it. Let Shepherd do it."

In a cold, hard voice, Migliardo said, "Tow him over here, Barr, or we'll tie him around your neck."

"No!" Barr whimpered. "No!"

"Take him, Barr," Holloway said in a thin voice.

Slowly Barr drifted back to the bunk. Moving with great caution, so that he did not touch the body, he released the belt on either side. Slowly he pulled on one strap. The body rolled in the air and followed him. Suddenly the eyelids sprang open. The sightless eyes stared accusingly at Barr.

Barr dropped the strap as if it burned his hand and threw his arm up in front of his face. "Ted!" he screamed. "I didn't do it!"

The body drifted to Jelinek, who was clinging to the fireman's pole. He caught it by one arm. "Barr!"

Moving like a man asleep, Barr turned and pushed himself toward Jelinek. He caught the pole and then took the belt strap in his hand. He went through the hole.

The others followed—Jelinek, Migliardo, Holloway. They formed a circle around the pole. Jelinek straightened out the body so that it lay at their feet. The eyelids refused to close.

Migliardo said, "How about Shepherd?"

"He's on watch," Jelinek said.

Migliardo cleared his throat. " 'Man that is born of woman,' " he said softly, " 'hath but a short time to live, and is full of misery. He cometh up and is cut down like a flower; he fleeth as it were a shadow, and never continueth in one stay. . . .' "

They bowed their heads for a moment.

Jelinek looked up. "Get into your suit, Barr."

Barr turned blindly, opened a locker, and put on his suit automatically. When he was ready, Migliardo had the airlock door open.

Jelinek said, "Take the body out. Give it a good shove."

Barr picked up the trailing belt strap and moved clumsily into the airlock. The body stirred. Jelinek guided it into the cylinder.

The clang of the door was a somber note of finality. They stared at it for a moment and then, one by one, they swung along the pole to the living deck.

Holloway turned immediately to one of the ports, opened it, and looked out. "I don't see anything."

Migliardo asked, "What are we going to do with Barr? We can't let him go free."

"Vengeance?" Jelinek asked.

"Common sense. Do you suppose there was really something wrong with his suit?"

Jelinek shook his head gloomily. "Too easy. And too ironic. Justice doesn't work so directly. No, Barr was the only homicidal personality we had aboard. And we're going to have to live with him for the next two years or so. Jolly."

"Can't you—" Migliardo's voice broke, "put him away?"

"No, I can't. I can remember when he was my best friend. He might be that again." Jelinek's voice dropped. "Barr didn't kill Ted; space did it. How can you condemn a man for something you've considered, rationally, cold-bloodedly, yourself? Could you kill Barr?"

Migliardo hesitated. "No."

"None of us could."

Holloway said urgently, "I don't see them. There's something wrong. There's nothing out there."

The airlock door suddenly clanged. Jelinek looked around the room and then floated quickly to Barr's locker, opened it, and pulled out a small pipe wrench. "Go lie in your bunk, Burt. Hide this. Use it if necessary."

Holloway stared at Jelinek with frightened eyes and then moved to his bunk. He adjusted his straps to the rings and stretched out, the wrench along the leg nearest the wall.

Barr had removed his suit. He came cautiously along the pole. "Did you shove off the body?"

"Yes." Barr's eyes shifted to the open port.

"Mig," Jelinek said quietly. "Check."

Migliardo looked once at Barr and left.

"Barr," Jelinek said, "what are we going to do with you?"

Barr's muscular hands flexed nervously. "I don't know."

"You might kill again."

"No!" Barr shouted. "I wouldn't. I was only—I swear to you, Emil, I didn't kill him."

"Iron," Jelinek said, shaking his head, "how can we believe you? How can we trust you?"

He pushed himself away from the wall with one hand. He floated toward Barr. Barr shoved himself back. "Don't try anything!" he said wildly. "I'm warning you. I'll do something. I'll —I'll take care of all of you. I'll kill you, Emil, if you touch me." His fists were doubled as his back touched the wall close to Holloway's bunk. He started drifting back.

Jelinek moved his hand. The needle of the syrette gleamed.

"You're trying to poison me!" Barr screamed. "I'll kill you— all of you. I'll—"

Holloway brought the wrench down on Barr's head. It made a dull, hollow sound. Barr's eyes rolled back in his head. His body twitched once, and then it was still, floating in the air.

Jelinek said, "Thanks, Burt," and began towing Barr toward his bunk. He snapped Barr's belt onto the rings. He went to his locker and got a roll of adhesive tape. Carefully he taped Barr's wrists to the framework of the bunk, winding the tape around and around. Then he selected a vein on the inside of Barr's elbow and injected the contents of the syrette.

The airlock door clanged. In a few moments Migliardo came into the room. He took in the situation at a glance. Jelinek was rubbing disinfectant into the cut on Barr's head.

Migliardo said, "He stuffed Ted's body in among the sounding missiles. I shoved it off. I see you took care of—the situation."

Jelinek looked up angrily. "For how long? My morphine will last for thirty days. What do we do then?"

"Maybe when we reach Mars—" Migliardo stopped.

"Can we trust him then?"

Migliardo shrugged helplessly. "You're the doctor."

Barr's eyelids flickered. "Mama," he said.

Migliardo turned to the pole. "I'm going to talk to Shepherd."

The deck was silent then except for the voice of a mistreated child saying, "Mama."

IX

When the lights came on, Faust was blinking. "Those poor, damn bastards," he said softly. It was almost a prayer.

Danton was staring blankly at the screen, his hands clenched in his lap. "I can't take any more," he said hoarsely.

Faust said, "Don't blame yourself, Amos."

Danton looked at Faust with eyes filled with guilt and horror. "I sent them out, Jim. Me. I sent them into that. I killed Ted. I made Iron into a homicidal maniac."

"I picked them," Lloyd said.

Faust said, "Nobody's responsible. It's space. Those men went because they had to, just as you came out, Amos, because you had to. Any new environment is hungry. Men tame it by dying for it. Men died for the Western Hemisphere, to tame the Antarctic, to develop atomic power, to build skyscrapers and roads. Men died to build the Little Wheel and the Big Wheel. Space is hungry, too. And men stick their heads in its mouth because they're men."

"Too old," Danton said, shaking his white head, "I grew old too soon." He turned and walked erectly out of the room.

"Thanks," Lloyd said quietly.

"You think I didn't mean it?"

"I know you meant it. But that wasn't all you meant. You didn't tell him we'd have to give up if the *Santa Maria* doesn't make it."

"He knows it," Faust said.

"Another tape?"

"No," Faust said. He smiled wearily. "Like Amos, I can't take any more." He tried to sound cheerful. "Well, maybe they'll make it. There's still five of them."

"Five?"

"Sure. Barr, Jelinek, Holloway, Shepherd, Migliardo."

"Jim," Lloyd said, "only five men went aboard that ship when it started for Mars. One of them is dead."

"But there's five!"

"What does Shepherd look like?"

Faust said thoughtfully, "He's got a beard. Rather tired, deep-set eyes—"

"How do you know, Jim? You've never seen him."

Faust looked startled. "I must have. I can almost see him now —He must have been a stowaway. That's why he wasn't in the first few films. Behind that sealed panel—?"

"Jim," Lloyd repeated, "you've never seen him."

Faust rubbed his eyes hard with his knuckles. "You're right. He was on the control deck the whole tape. Hallucination? How do you account for it?"

Lloyd shrugged helplessly. "I know the seed, but I can't account for the flower. There's that safety factor we told them about. And there was a posthypnotic suggestion we gave them: if they were ever in desperate trouble, there would be help."

"Barr thought you were tricky."

"No trick, Jim. It's real. There's help. But we never expected it to take this form." Lloyd's jaw tightened. "Come on, Jim, I'll show you your cabin."

He led Faust down the spoke to the other side of the wheel and the cabin he had once occupied when he had first come out.

"Amos is having some dinner sent in for the two of you," Lloyd said. "He'll expect you in his cabin next door at 1800. Anything you'd like?"

Faust shook his head. As Lloyd turned toward the spoke, Faust said in a puzzled voice, "If I never saw Shepherd, how did I know what he looked like?"

Lloyd said, "I wish you could answer that question for me."

The hot, steamy hydroponics room was on the other side of the Wheel beyond the air-conditioning unit. A wide, flat tank of green-scummed water took up most of the floor space. The algae in the tank were absorbing carbon dioxide from the Wheel's air and producing fifty times their own volume of oxygen every hour.

Beyond the big tank was a smaller one in which flowers and vegetables were growing. An old man was puttering among them —not really old, but old by spaceman's standards. He was fifty.

Lloyd saluted. "General Kovac!"

Kovac waved carelessly at him. "Relax, Lloyd. I'm just the gardener now. If Amos and I hadn't been young officers together, he'd never have let me retire to this job and you know it." His wrinkled face creased in a smile. "Thanks, though."

Lloyd smiled back. "I wondered, Max, if maybe you could spare me some flowers."

Kovac picked up a box wrapped in thick padding. "All boxed and insulated. Gardenias, Amos said."

Lloyd took the box and looked down at it, biting his lower lip. "Gardenias. You and Amos—"

"Shut up now," Kovac snapped. "Don't want to hear any more about it. Neither does Amos. Tell Terry not to be a fool."

"Thanks, Max. I'll try."

The recreation room of the cottage was empty. Lloyd wondered where the boys were. He unwrapped the insulation from the box and opened it. The gardenias were as fresh and white as if they had been just picked on Earth. Lloyd looked down at them, took a deep breath, and lifted the door to the living room.

Terry looked up as he came down the ladder. She was ironing a frilly dress. She started to say something and stopped. Lloyd dropped the last few feet and landed lightly. "For you," he said, presenting the gardenias.

Terry looked at the flowers, and her face crumpled. Blindly, she held out her hand to take them. She raised them to her face and breathed in their fragrance.

"Oh, Lloyd," she said. "They're beautiful."

Lloyd said, "Not as beautiful as you." His voice was husky.

Terry's face was flushed. "I don't know what to say."

"Don't say anything. If I brought you flowers every time I wanted to say 'I love you' there'd be no room in the cottage for

us. I do love you, Terry. More than anything. More than my job.
If you want to go Inside—I'll go with you."

"Oh, Lloyd!" She brushed her eyes with the back of one hand.
"I do sound like a fool, don't I? You know I wouldn't take you
away. I just—I just want to feel needed."

"If you should leave me," Lloyd said, "the stars might as well
fall out of the sky."

She looked at him searchingly. "I almost believe you mean
that. Oh, I will believe it. Lloyd!" She put her arms around him
and squeezed him tightly to her. "I'm so happy."

He could feel her heart beating against his chest, hard and fast.
He thought, *If only I wasn't a psychologist, if I could stop analyzing
myself and everyone around me, if I could act blindly instead of always the
right way. Well,* he thought, *don't you love her? Yes. Yes!*

Her face was raised to his, her eyes closed. His mouth descended on hers, hard and demanding. Her lips parted.

When he raised his head the words were tumbling out, "Terry,
we're going to throw the nine cottages together with the tenth in
the middle for a recreation center. You'll have a chance to see the
other women oftener. There'll be dances, card parties, movies,
all kinds of get-togethers. We'll have a real community—"

She put a finger across his lips and murmured, "That's fine,
honey. That's wonderful." He kissed her again.

With that communion of marriage that sometimes makes ex-
planations unnecessary, he said irrelevantly, "What about the
boys?"

"They're taking a nap," she whispered, clinging to him.

He picked her up and carried her easily toward the bedroom.
She opened her eyes and whispered, "The iron, honey."

Swearing, he stormed back across the room, yanked out the
cord with a jerk, and stamped back toward the bedroom.

Terry sighed. She was smiling.

X

One hundred and ninety-seven days out. The *Santa Maria* swept on through space with its animate and inanimate cargo. Earth was far behind now. Mars was appreciably closer—it showed a perceptible disk.

Holloway was lying in his bunk. He was propped up by a ripped piece of padding against the pressure of his belt so that he could stare out the port. He was much thinner. His eyes were burned holes in the blank sheet of his face.

Barr was taped to the framework of his bunk. Migliardo clung with one leg to a stanchion beside it. He was trying to feed Barr cut-up steak from a covered dish with a pair of tongs. Migliardo put a bite of meat into Barr's mouth. Barr spat it out.

"You're trying to poison me!" Barr screamed. "I ain't gonna eat anything! You're trying to get rid of me."

"Iron," Migliardo said patiently, grabbing the bit of meat out of the air and holding it in his hand, "you saw me get the meat out of the freezer. You saw me put it in the range. You saw me take it out and bring it over here. If you don't eat, you'll die for sure."

Barr's body flopped in the air as he struggled against the tape that bound him to the bunk, but he could get no leverage. Even Barr was gaunt. "I ain't gonna eat!" he shouted. "And I ain't gonna die. One of these days I'm gonna get loose, and I'm gonna kill everyone of you—you and Emil and Burt and Ted and— Everybody but Shepherd. He's nice to me. . . ."

Migliardo sighed and pushed away. He scraped the food into the garbage ejector and floated to the pole, Barr's hysterical obscenities following inexorably. He pulled himself to the control deck. Jelinek was sitting in the navigator's chair. He was sighting at Mars through the telescope.

"Emil," Migliardo said.

Jelinek jumped and banged his eye on the eyepiece of the telescope. He looked around, rubbing his eye.

"What are you doing?"

Jelinek grinned sheepishly. "Practicing my navigation. Burt isn't going to be much help, and if something should happen—"

"To me?" Migliardo nodded. "Good idea. I guess I should practice my piloting. But I never was much of a pilot. Anyway, there's Shepherd."

They looked at each other steadily, considering all the possibilities. Migliardo's face relaxed. "We're going to get through, hey, Emil?"

"You and me and Shepherd."

"You know, I was never what you would call a good Catholic, but I've been praying lately. Shepherd and me. Maybe it's helped."

"Maybe. But don't forget that the Lord helps those who help themselves. How are the engines?"

"Number two rigid-mount is pitted, but it should stand up under one more firing easily—two if we're lucky."

Barr was still screaming. Migliardo listened for a moment. He said, "I don't know how much longer I can take it, Emil. Night and day that goes on. You can't get away from it. Doesn't he ever sleep?"

"He takes catnaps all day long. We don't notice. We should be like Burt. He doesn't notice anything." Jelinek studied Migliardo. "He's bound to weaken. He hasn't eaten for a week, and if we tried to feed him intravenously like Burt, he'd tear out the scoop."

Migliardo listened to Barr and shivered. "Anything we can do?"

"I ran out of morphine a month ago; reserpine doesn't help. Besides, he thinks he's being poisoned."

Migliardo rubbed his mouth nervously. "It's like taking care of a baby, feeding him, washing him, bringing him bedpans. Only a baby can't talk."

"I'd spell you, Mig—you know that. But it only makes him worse. He's more afraid of me."

Migliardo bit his lower lip. "Sure. Sorry. Sometimes it just gets too much for me—" He turned his head to listen. "There! He stopped." His expression changed. "That was quick. Too quick. I'll go check."

He slid along the pole. There was a brief period of silence and then Migliardo's horrified shouts, "Emil! For God's sake, Emil!"

There was a red haze in the living deck. Red droplets floated in the air. Barr was lying in his bunk, his jugular vein still spurting blood into the air. Jelinek caught the bunk's framework and pressed his hand to the three-inch, horizontal gash in Barr's throat, but the pumping had already slowed. It stopped as Jelinek fumbled for the artery. Barr was dead.

Barr's eyes were open. In them was a mixture of terror and hatred. The door to the locker beside his head was standing open. His right arm was free. In his right hand was a razor-sharp clasp knife. The knife and the hand were covered with blood. His whole body was bathed in blood.

So was Migliardo, who clung to the bunk beside Jelinek. Between red smears, his face was white.

"It's all over, Mig," Jelinek said quietly. "Better clean up."

Migliardo said slowly, "I never knew a man had so much blood in him." He seemed unable to move.

Jelinek pushed him toward the shower stall. "Go sponge off. And put those shorts in the ejector." When he heard the brief hiss of water from the stall, Jelinek drifted to his bunk and took a towel from his locker. Slowly he wiped the blood from his hand. "Did you see anything, Burt?"

Holloway was staring out the port. "No," he said distantly, "I haven't seen anything. Only the stars. Earth is still a long ways off. Sometimes I don't think we will ever get there. I think maybe

Earth is just a dream I dreamed one night, and there isn't really an Earth at all. Or maybe I'm just a dream someone else is dreaming. Then it wouldn't matter. Dreams don't matter." His voice trailed away.

The red fog was gone, sucked away through the air-conditioning intakes, but many spherical red drops still floated aimlessly in the air. Methodically Jelinek slapped at them with the towel. When there were only minute droplets that air movement would take care of, Jelinek tied the stained towel around Barr's neck and closed the staring eyes.

Migliardo came out of the shower stall, clean, naked, and very pale. The room was oppressively silent as he went to his locker for a pair of shorts.

Jelinek said, "Barr's better off now. He was incurable, even if we could have got him back to Earth. Let's get him to the storage deck."

They towed the body to the pole and along it to the deck next to the airlock door. "Shepherd?" Jelinek said.

They stood there, Jelinek and Migliardo, their heads bowed above Barr's restless body. After a few moments they looked up. Jelinek said, "Thanks, Shepherd. Mig?"

Migliardo nodded silently and began putting on his suit.

"When you get back," Jelinek said, "you and Shepherd better clean up the splashes. Get rid of the bunk canvas through the ejector. I'm going back on watch."

Migliardo nodded again and lowered his helmet over his head. Jelinek adjusted the wing nuts and then went along the pole toward the control deck. As he passed the living deck, he looked slowly around the deck and frowned. Then he continued along the pole.

XI

Without turning on the lights, Lloyd said to the two heads between him and the screen, "The two hundred and sixtieth day tape has just arrived. Shall we run it?"

Danton said hoarsely, "Yes. It will tell the story."

Faust said, "Run it."

The scene flickered on the screen.

XII

Two hundred and sixty days out. In front of the *Santa Maria*, Mars was a vast disk, glowing red and white and green. It was 8,500 miles away. The canals were clearly visible, natural faults in the Martian crust through which fog rolled from the south pole. The surface seemed to rotate with ever-increasing speed.

Ignition was sixty-four minutes away.

Migliardo was sitting in the table slings reading a book bound in black leather. It was a Bible.

Jelinek was floating beside Holloway's bunk. The navigator's eyes were closed. His chest scarcely seemed to move. Jelinek held his wrist and counted to himself. Finally he nodded in the silence and glanced at the clock. "Sixty-two minutes until ignition. We'd better get busy, Mig."

Migliardo did not look up. "Shepherd will take care of it."

"Mig—" Jelinek began and hesitated. "I've been going through the log, Mig. I can't find any mention of Shepherd before one hundred and twelve days out."

Migliardo shrugged. "You made a mistake."

"No. I was surprised. I checked twice. Mig, what does Shepherd look like?"

Migliardo kept on reading. "You know what he looks like. He's got a beard. Sad, deep-set eyes—"

"A sort of towel wrapped around his hips?"

"Of course not," Migliardo said. "He wears khaki shorts like the rest of us."

Jelinek sighed and drifted toward Migliardo. "So he does. It's amazing he should look the same to both of us."

"Why? That's how he looks."

Jelinek caught the edge of the table and brought his face close to Migliardo's. "Because, Mig, he really isn't there."

Migliardo looked up sharply. "Don't say that, Emil! We're jittery enough as it is. Don't you crack on us!"

"Think back, Mig," Jelinek said softly. "A long, long way. Back to the moment when we boarded this ship from the Little Wheel. Phillips had said good-by, Danton had said good-by; we were all alone, now, and the taxi had taken us to the *Santa Maria*, and we were there where we would live, some of us, for two and a half years. Who was there, Mig?"

Migliardo's forehead furrowed. "You and me and Iron and Burt and Ted and—and—" He looked at Jelinek with wide, dark eyes. "Shepherd wasn't there."

"When did he get on, Mig?"

"How could he get on after we had started, Emil? He wasn't there and now he is. That's all."

"Guess for me, Mig. What is Shepherd?"

"You guess."

"I'll tell you something else I've been checking on. The supplies. Just the two of us have been eating, Mig. Just the three of us, counting Burt, have been breathing and drinking. Shepherd doesn't eat or drink or breathe.

"What would I call him? A mass hallucination, whatever that might be. The manifestation of a deep-felt need triggered by certain instructions given us and perhaps by a posthypnotic suggestion. But I don't think it was planned."

Migliardo said, "That's just witch doctor stuff, Emil."

Jelinek nodded. "True. But the subconscious plays some funny tricks. Now you guess for me."

"You're wrong about the first mention of Shepherd. What about the face Burt saw through the port? What about the stowaway Ted saw?"

"That would make him something—not human."

"Whatever he is, he's not human. How do we know what waits for man in interplanetary space?"

"That's not your best guess, Mig."

"My best guess isn't a guess; it's a faith. Why do we call him Shepherd? Did he tell us? Did one of us name him? Or was it something else that just came to us?"

"You tell me."

Migliardo said softly, " 'The Lord is my shepherd; I shall not want. He maketh me to lie down in green pastures: he leadeth me beside the still waters. He restoreth my soul: he leadeth me in the paths of righteousness for his name's sake. Yea, though I walk through the valley of the shadow of death, I will fear no evil.' "

"That's a good guess, Mig," Jelinek said slowly. "Maybe better than mine. It has all the stigmata of a psychological truth and contact points with experience—the still waters and the valley of the shadow of death. I wish I wasn't such a skeptic. I'd like to pray with you and Shepherd. The trouble is—I haven't seen Shepherd lately."

"Emil—!" Migliardo began. "I've been wanting to tell you something for a long time."

"Confession?" Jelinek asked gently.

"In more ways than one. I killed Barr."

"I know you did. The tape that held his wrist was cut, not torn. He couldn't have cut it until he had the knife, and he couldn't get the knife until his hand was free. Besides, Barr would never have committed suicide. He would have cut loose and come after us."

Migliardo put his hand across his eyes. "He was my friend."

"It was what he would have wanted a friend to do—if he had been sane enough to know a friend. There are none of us innocent, Mig." Jelinek looked at the clock. "Twenty-five minutes until ignition."

An expression of concern crossed Migliardo's face. "If Shepherd isn't real, then we can't—He's on the control deck, isn't he, Emil?"

Jelinek frowned. "I don't know. I haven't seen him lately."

Migliardo was already pulling his legs free of the slings. He swung along the pole hastily and stopped with his head just beyond the partition. "Shepherd! Emil, he's gone!" He came back along the pole and searched the living deck with dark, frightened eyes. "Shepherd! Shepherd!"

He kept on moving along the pole until he reached the storage deck. "Shepherd!" he called. And despairingly, "Shepherd?"

Suddenly Jelinek moved. "Mig!" He leaped toward the pole.

"Shepherd!" Migliardo called once more and then the airlock door clanged shut. Before Jelinek could reach the door, he heard the hissing sound of air escaping.

Jelinek turned, gnawing his mustache, and opened the lockers along the wall. Migliardo's suit was there. So were the other four. Jelinek looked at the airlock door and said softly, "So long, Mig. I hope you find him."

With a great weariness, he pulled himself along a pole to the living deck. There was a great silence in the ship, a silence alive and unbearable. Jelinek looked at the clock. Twenty minutes until ignition. He looked at Holloway. He could barely see his chest move.

"The silence," he muttered. "That's the worst."

He floated to Holloway and felt his pulse again. He frowned, turned to a cabinet set in the wall, and withdrew one end of a coil of plastic tubing. There was a needle on the end of it. Jelinek found a vein on Holloway's arm, inserted the needle, and turned on the tiny motor that forced the sugar solution drop by drop into Holloway's vein.

Jelinek floated to his locker, opened it, and removed a hypodermic already filled with a clear liquid. He studied it for a moment, looked at Holloway, and then looked at the clock. Fifteen minutes until ignition.

He tossed the hypodermic back into the locker and slammed the door. He pulled himself swiftly along the pole to the control deck and strapped himself into the captain's chair. His eyes ran over the master controls, his fingers hovering over the control board. Ten minutes more. Not enough time.

Suddenly there came the sound of pumps churning and water surging. Jelinek looked down at his fingers. They had not touched the control board.

There was a series of small explosions somewhere in the ship, like firecrackers in the distance on the Fourth of July. Jelinek listened. Somewhere motors started and flywheels turned. Mars slowly began to slip away from the astrogation dome as the ship turned. Through a porthole in the side Jelinek could see a giant white globe floating gently away. It was an empty fuel tank.

Jelinek smiled suddenly and took his hand away from the control board. "Ah, there, Shepherd!"

Mars appeared in the living-deck porthole by Holloway's bunk. It filled it completely, a spinning red, white, and green sphere.

Holloway pushed himself upright in his bunk, his eyes open, a shaky finger pointing. From that arm the plastic tube dangled and swung. "Earth!" Holloway shouted. His eyelids flickered. His eyes rolled back. Slowly, under the pressure of his belt straps, he sank toward the bunk. When he was parallel with it again, his chest was not moving.

"Burt!" Jelinek called from the control deck. He did not call again. The speaker imbedded in the stanchion by Holloway's bunk was utterly silent. "You weren't so bad a navigator, Burt. After all, Columbus never knew he had discovered the New World."

He stared around the room, watching the lights winking and changing color, the dials turning, the ship silhouette on the artificial horizon slowly changing shape. The control deck was alive....

He listened to the sounds it made, the cluckings and the tickings, the whines and the creaks. He smelled the air, all the mingled, ineradicable stinks of men sweating and breathing and eliminating, as if he were smelling it for the first time in a long while, and the smell was sweet. He ran his hands along the chair arms.

He put his hand over the control panel and pressed the button marked "Air Conditioner—Stop." One of the sounds—a whisper —was no more. He then pressed the button beside it: "Air— Eject." A red light sprang to life on the control board; a thin whistling noise began.

"Lloyd," Jelinek said softly, "I suppose you're watching. You never told me, but I guess that's the way it had to be. I hope you've learned something." He chuckled; it was almost a happy sound. "Perhaps to pick a better psychologist."

His voice changed, sobered. "I'm sorry, Lloyd. I couldn't face it—the loneliness and the silence. I think the silence was worst of all.

"Tell Amos—the crew was a failure—but the ship was a success. And tell him—there'll be a ship—out here—in good working order—with fuel and supplies—if anyone—ever makes it. . . ."

After a little the whistling stopped and the air was gone. On the control deck two blind eyes looked out at the circling stars and two deaf ears listened to the sound of rocket engines screaming. . . .

XIII

The silence in the little room was almost as unbearable as that aboard the *Santa Maria*. Lloyd had forgotten to turn on the lights. Nobody noticed; nobody said anything. When Lloyd finally remembered, Danton was still clutching the arms of his chair in knuckle-whitened hands, tears rolling down his face unashamedly.

Faust was shading his eyes with his hands. "So," he said finally,

"I must prepare for the worst. There is little time."

Lloyd's voice sounded strange to him. "What could you do with two years?"

Faust looked up quickly. His eyes, too, were damp. "Where would we get two years?"

"The ship isn't expected back until then."

"How could you fake it that long?"

Lloyd said methodically, "The *Santa Maria* has taken up its orbit around Mars, six hundred and twenty miles up. It will be sending back telemetered reports from its telescopic examination of the surface, from its sounding missiles, and there are even several missiles equipped to land on Mars, conduct geological explorations within a limited radius, analyze samples, and telemeter back their findings.

"That was our safety factor—apart from special, unlikely emergencies such as that meteor damage, the ship alone was capable of making the trip and doing the job. Subconsciously the men realized it. They personified the ship; they called it Shepherd. It wasn't enough. . . ."

Lloyd stopped, then began again. "The ship's reports will give us something to announce from time to time. As far as the crew is concerned, we don't *have* to know about it. If we need more time still, we can announce that the ship will wait for the next favorable opportunity to return."

"Too many people know. You couldn't keep it a secret."

Lloyd sighed. "We're used to keeping secrets, aren't we, Amos? The men who are working on the tapes will be here until we're ready to release the information. They have years of work ahead of them."

"Maybe it could be done," Faust admitted, "but why? Do you think you can pick a better crew—one that will succeed where those men failed?"

Danton's voice was cold and harsh.

"Those were the best!"

"Then where are you going to get the spacemen?" Faust asked gently.

"We aren't," Danton said fiercely. "Turn on that still of the *Santa Maria!*" The picture of the ship appeared on the screen, silvery white and fragile. "There's your spaceman. That's all there will ever be—packed solid with usable stuff. No neuroses, no tummy aches, no weakness, no indecision, no space-madness. It doesn't need oxygen, food, or water, medicine, sterilizers, entertainment, and the rest of the junk we have to have to survive. Just servo-mechanisms and telemetering devices. Robots. There's your spaceman. He can travel anywhere, sense almost everything, do almost anything, and never worry about coming back. . . ."

Faust shook his head.

"No, Amos," Lloyd said, "it won't do. As a research tool, it's fine. As a symbol it just won't do. Men's representatives, meaningful representatives, must be living, breathing, fearful men like themselves. They've got to be men doing something the people who are left behind think they could have done, given the opportunity—men whose doings give them glory. You told me that once, Amos. Do you remember? I've never forgotten."

Faust said slowly. "How long do you need?"

"Eight years maybe. Ten years for sure."

"That's a long time."

"Mars will wait."

"Where are you going to get them," Faust asked, "these spacemen?"

Lloyd knew that he had his ten years. "If we can't find them readymade, we'll have to make them ourselves."

XIV

In the airlock of the cottage, Lloyd extracted himself from his suit, picked up his insulated box, and opened the inner door. Two squirming bundles of exuberance launched themselves at him, plastic helmets on their dark heads, ray guns in their hands, shouting their welcomes, "Daddy, you're home early! Play spaceman with us! Hey, Daddy?"

"Hello," Lloyd said gently. "Hello, spacemen."

The Joy Ride

I

And if any is unhappy, remember that he is for himself;
for God made all men to enjoy felicity and peace.

EPICTETUS

D'GLAS M'GREGOR met the Duplicate in the corridor connecting the motor pool and the elevator bank. It would have been easy enough to recognize if D'glas's mind had been properly disengaged from his autonomic nervous system, but he was well past it, frowning darkly, before he whirled to the control panel.

The corridor wall opened at his touch. For a fraction of a second, the indicator light behind it was steady. Then the Duplicate began to move at a speed of 200 kilometers an hour.

D'glas's fingers blurred as they flashed to the controls. The far panel dropped, cutting off the Duplicate from the motor pool and the surface of Venus. Instantly, it reversed directions. It was moving back toward D'glas at the same incredible speed when the second panel dropped.

For a moment the indicator stood still, burning brightly. Then it was off.

D'glas sighed. The trap had failed again. . . .

The rain was falling on Venus in an endless flood; the carbon dioxide atmosphere twenty times as dense as that on earth made hurricanes seem tame and flung the deluge about like bullets and guillotines. But even such torrents hadn't reached the 600° surface for a century. By then, at the poles at least, the temperature had dropped below the boiling point of water, and the carbon dioxide content of the air had dropped perceptibly as it was bound into carbon compounds and into sedimentary rock. The rain had been falling for two hundred years. It would fall for two hundred more before it began to slacken.

By then there would be seas and lakes and ponds where free water had never existed. Cleansed by fire and oxygen of its deadly ingredients of carbon dioxide and acids, breathable for the first time with free oxygen, the atmosphere would be completely changed.

And one day the clouds would break up, and the sun would shine down upon a Venus unveiled, a world transformed by Man.

Venus had been stillborn. Almost a twin of Earth, it had been embalmed at birth, shrouded in stifling clouds of carbon dioxide, hydrochloric and hydrofluoric acids.

Beneath those miles of poisonous clouds, Man found a desert where nothing lived, where nothing could live. The vital ingredients were missing: free water, free oxygen. What it offered were unbearable pressures and burning temperatures.

The colonists dug deep beneath the surface to escape the pressure, the heat, and the vicious thermodynamic forces of the atmosphere, and then they set methodically about the task of changing a world.

Diatoms had been created and released to live in the clouds, to float in rich winds of carbon dioxide and convert it into free oxygen and carbon compounds which, on their deaths, would fertilize the land below.

Sponge platinum supplied the catalytic action. Venus itself supplied the power. Every lightning bolt released water and fertilizing nitrates upon the land. And Man himself was busy in great, lumbering combines which crawled the desert, chewing up sand and stone and leaving behind, to soak up the rain, soil rich with fertilizers, long-chain proteins, genetically designed microorganisms, earthworms, and seed.

In spots that grew steadily, Venus began to assume a second veil, a veil that lived, a veil of green. And the grasses and plants and trees took carbon dioxide from the air, bound the carbon into their stalks and trunks and leaves, and released free oxygen to the atmosphere.

It took Man four hundred years to conquer the relatively benign North American continent. In the same time he would change Venus's alien, poisonous nature. Already he had tamed her, sweetened her breath, softened her hard bosom. Now he was making her fertile.

In another two hundred years she would be as fair as Earth.

Driven raindrops swirled suddenly against the lens above. In the room below, the scene blurred; rain seemed to stream down the repeater window. As it cleared, a long, blinding chain of lightning danced along the horizon.

Perry closed his eyes. "So near," he murmured. "And yet so far. All right, D'glas, wake up."

"I'm awake," D'glas said. "You've got the story?" He straightened up in the diagnostic chair, rubbing his arm where the hypodermic jet had irritated the skin.

Perry was seventy years old, and his middle-aged face had settled into wise, tolerant lines and creases. But now it was troubled. "There's no doubt. It was a Duplicate. Guy Reeder, the lay hedonist, was on a combine at the time."

"That's how I recognized it. I had just left him—"

"We know," Brian broke in, motioning at the chair with the mouthpiece of his pacifier in a gesture that summed up the whole, subconscious interrogatory. He was a few years younger than Perry and perhaps a few years less patient. He pointed the pacifier at D'glas. "And in a foul temper you left him. Which is why you were almost too late in recognizing the Duplicate. Boy, you need treatment."

Besides D'glas, there were three of them in the room. Perry, Brian, and Floyd—as dissimilar as three men can be, but hedonists all. What government there was on Venus existed here. Whatever these men decided in their wisdom would be the concurrent decision of three million colonists.

Three hedonists, and D'glas. He felt outnumbered and alone.

"I was angry, I admit," he said grudgingly. "To me the combine work is boring and unrewarding. And when Guy tried to convince me that this was modification of reality in the hedonic sense, I quit and came back."

"What could be greater modification?" Floyd asked quietly from the corner, his dark face shadowed and anonymous.

"To apply it here is casuistry," D'glas flashed back. "Our work is drudgery, not pleasure."

"Happiness comes from inside," Brian said soberly. "What hedonics gives us are the techniques with which to make necessity a virtue, with which to make the unavoidable a pleasure. 'What cannot be cured must be endured, and what must be endured should be enjoyed.' "

" 'When rape becomes inevitable—' " D'glas growled. "I'll quote Morgan to you verse by verse. I know what he brought us from Earth a century ago. But your hedonism is little different from my stoicism. There should be more for Man than grubbing in the dirt."

"I would like to point out," Perry said quietly, "that the decision is not whether we should or should not grub in the dirt, but whether we will be permitted to do so if we wish."

As quickly as it had come, D'glas's anger ebbed. This was a good society. There had never been a better. A man had a right to do anything he wished, to be anything he wished except unhappy. And society must be conceded the ultimate right to outlaw those emotions which are destructive of the society itself. An unhappy man is a deadly focus of social disintegration.

It was, D'glas thought, a significant comment on this society that in the middle of the most desperate struggle of its existence it could concern itself with the hedonic condition of a single citizen.

"We have assumed," Perry continued, "that the Duplicates were a threat. The threat has become imminent. If we learn anything from this incident, it is this: the Duplicates are telepathic. Let's re-examine the tape."

Perry pressed the side of the window frame. Within it, the surface of Venus vanished, replaced by a dim corridor. A man was walking away from them. As they watched him, the man, without a backward glance, began to run.

"You had just opened the control panel," Perry said.

The Duplicate did not begin clumsily, as men do, building up momentum. It started at high speed, its legs churning like pistons, blurring even on the high-speed film. Ahead, a panel fell, closing the end of the corridor.

Without hesitation the Duplicate jumped, landing with both feet against the panel, absorbing momentum with bending knees. When they snapped back, they propelled the Duplicate back the way it had come, its legs flashing before they touched the floor. Now they could see its face.

It was the Duplicate of Guy Reeder.

The second panel dropped, completing the fourth wall of the cell. The camera shifted. They were inside the cell with the Duplicate. For an instant it stood frozen. The next moment the only trace of it was a cloud of disintegrating particles.

"That," Perry sighed, "was taken at a speed of one million frames a second."

"Same spectroscopic analysis?"

"Exactly," Floyd said quietly. "It is not human. There is, generally, a higher percentage of metal in the Duplicate."

Perry returned the window to its view of the rain-swept plains of Venus. "The first one was reported two days ago—almost five hundred hours. This is the fifth one. We have trapped two. Both instantly blew themselves into their constituent atoms. There must be others among us which have not been detected."

Brian removed the pacifier from his mouth. "Too soon. We are not ready for contact with aliens."

"Aliens? You're sure?" D'glas asked quickly.

Brian shrugged. "Their abilities aren't human."

"The percentage of metal suggests that they are mechs," Floyd added. "And the self-destruction, too. There may be alien races which can blow themselves to pieces at will, but I doubt it."

"A humanoid mech?" D'glas said, puzzled. "Why?"

"To pass among us unsuspected," Perry said.

"What for? They haven't done anything."

"So far. Perhaps. In our society it is difficult to know when changes occur. At this moment we are under observation."

Brian and Floyd nodded.

"What the next stage will be," Perry went on calmly, "is impossible to guess, but it will not be favorable to a continuation of our society and of our way of life."

Again the hedonists nodded.

"What are we going to do, then?" D'glas demanded, his dark, young face scowling.

"The first thing," Perry said, without changing inflection, "is to make certain we all are human."

While he was speaking, the partitions were falling. Hedonic reflexes brought D'glas out of the diagnostic chair without hesitation, but it was too late. Already he was locked into a small metal room. It vibrated briefly.

Before he could sit down again, the partitions rose silently. Perry and Brian were looking at the corner where Floyd had been sitting. It was empty. The chair had disappeared. So had the rubberized flooring down to the steel beneath. The wall was scorched and black.

"They are determined," Perry said grimly, "that we shall not examine one. . . ."

Brian sucked on the pacifier reflectively before he removed it. "Did you expect this?"

"No," Perry admitted. "It was a precaution. To be truthful, I suspected you, Brian, if anyone. Your dependence on that pacifier seemed a little excessive."

"It's a small crutch which seems to be emotionally helpful in these troubled times," Brian said calmly. "In more plentiful times, I think I would have smoked tobacco in a pipe."

"And are the rest of us human?" D'glas asked.

"That's what the X rays indicate."

Brian got up lazily. "You don't mind if I check on you, do you, Perry?"

Perry smiled ruefully. "Not at all." He made room for Brian behind the desk. "It is unfortunate that Floyd's Duplicate didn't give us time to get a picture of its insides. But how can you trap a telepath?"

Brian studied the desk top, nodded, and moved back to his chair. "What about Floyd?"

"He's on his way here now—not that there's much we can do."

"Are we going to let them roam among us at will?" D'glas demanded. "Who knows what they may be planning?"

"Exactly," Brian said. "And so we cannot weigh the risk of preparing for it. Perhaps we could set up X-ray equipment in deserted corridors—deserted, of course, because the threat implicit is not yet dangerous enough to risk the death or injury of the general citizen."

"Beyond that," Perry said soberly, "we cannot go without losing that freedom of action and choice which is an integral part of our society. When the measures for the preservation of our society must, in themselves, destroy it, we must choose inaction."

Brian agreed gravely. "Wait and see. I am confident that hedonics can meet the test without additional preparation."

"Then we are going to do nothing?" D'glas exclaimed impatiently.

"As a group, yes," Perry said, unmoved. "As individuals, no. Each of us must act as his intellect and desires direct. That is the basis for our society, and it must so remain. But it would be desirable to warn the other colonies of our danger and ask their advice and help."

"We haven't heard from Ganymede and Callisto for a hundred years, from Mars for seventy-five," D'glas pointed out. "If they were going concerns, they would have contacted us by now."

"Have we contacted them?" Brian asked quietly. "Their job was more difficult than ours. We had only to change our atmosphere; they had to manufacture theirs. And yet even our society has been lean; we've had no fat for interplanetary jaunts."

"It was hedonics that brought us through," Perry added. "And we got hedonics only by accident. The original colonies had little use for such frivolities; it was equated with the oversensualism and overstimulation the colonists fled from. Morgan himself, who did so much to make applied hedonics a true science and then saw it perverted beyond control, came to Venus as a physician and teacher, not a hedonist. There are not many men like Morgan. Perhaps the other colonies were not so lucky."

"And perhaps the aliens conquered them first," D'glas said gloomily. "What about Earth?"

"Earth, too," Brian said, "although the case is not quite the same. Earth was never lean, and yet we lost touch with Earth one hundred years ago. She may be conquered. She may need help. It may even be possible that she can help us. I think some of us must make the effort."

"We have scavenged parts enough for four complete ships," Perry said. "One for each colony and one for Earth. After that there is no more, and it is questionable whether any of these will reach their destinations safely. But I think there will be volunteers."

"The Earth flight," D'glas heard himself saying. "I'll take it."

"Very well," Perry accepted gravely. "I wish you luck and happiness—for yourself and us."

D'glas didn't answer. He was stunned by what he had done. This is what the hedonists had wanted. Skillfully, they had worked him into risking himself on a wild and unpromising errand. Now it was too late to back out.

And yet, he felt a warm backlash of emotional release. For the first time he really understood the meaning of the word "voluntary." The job was there to be done. It should be done. Someone had to do it. He, D'glas M'Gregor, who was not happy to grub in the dirt, was the logical choice.

The result was pleasure. It was the hedonic reflex.

"Can you fly the ship?" Brian asked softly.

"I think so," D'glas said confidently. "I've done more complicated things in the exercises."

That was true. The hedonic training program developed muscular, sensory, and nervous discrimination and coordination side by side with mental agility and the all-important psychological control. It was complete.

"Good," Perry said. "You can start tomorrow. We have absolutely no time."

"Less than that," Floyd said from the doorway.

It was the real Floyd this time. Perry confirmed it by a glance at his desk.

"We're beginning to lose people," Floyd said quietly. "An accurate count is impossible in our society, but by my estimate more than one thousand persons have disappeared in the last two days."

"Where have they gone?" exclaimed D'glas.

Floyd shrugged. "Venus is a big world, and three million people don't make much impression on it. My guess is that the missing people are in the ships that brought the aliens—hidden underground, perhaps, in the boiling tropics. What worries me: have their places been taken by things that aren't human?"

II

O happiness! our being's end and aim!
Good pleasure, ease, content! whate'er thy name.
That something still which prompts the eternal sigh,
For which we bear to live, or dare to die.
                                        ALEXANDER POPE

It was a rocky landing, but a good one. Any landing a man can walk away from is a good one. D'glas walked away from this one.

The ship was not irreparably damaged. New first and second

stages, another load of fuel, and he might even be able to nurse it back to Venus.

He didn't worry about it. Ships stood tall all over the vast landing field, rusty missiles reaching high, aimed at the cloudless sky above. They hadn't flown for many years, but among them all there must be parts and equipment good for one more ship.

More important, he didn't want to consider the return trip. Not yet. The memory of the long, lonely voyage from Venus was still too fresh. Only his hedonic training had saved him from madness.

Now he stood with his two feet on the Earth and shivered. Earth was a mother no more.

Weight was on him again, feeling heavy and strange after the long weightlessness of the trip, and the air smelled flat and tasteless without the omnipresent odor of hydrogen chloride, and he was trapped between the concrete-covered soil and the naked sky, blue-clear and blazing.

It was horrible. It triggered subconscious and unsuspected reactions. He was afraid.

Ancient names that had almost passed out of the language of the Venusian colonists returned to him: agoraphobia, photophobia—He was exposed pitilessly upon a great plain; a giant eye stared down at him accusingly, watching, condemning. If he moved incautiously he might fall into the transparent blueness above, fall off the surface of the world into the terrible sky—

It was five minutes before he stopped shivering and the perspiration dried on his body. It took the hedonic exercises that long to re-emphasize the unity of mind and body, to damp the feedback of mind to senses. It took that long for the mind to accept the testimony of the senses and construct logical patterns out of it.

No clouds. That explained the blue emptiness above. That burning eye was the sun. The only direction he could fall was down.

D'glas turned to an inspection of the field. It was deserted.

More than that, abandoned. The concrete was cracked and uneven. Grass grew in long, green traceries. A nearby sapling was taller than D'glas. It had already begun the mighty destruction it would complete in maturity.

The warehouses and control towers that lined the city-side of the field had been built to endure, no doubt, but they were showing signs of long neglect. Their sides were stained, their windows broken. One had lost a wall; its roof leaned precariously over the void.

Over everything was a sensation of solitude, like an almost intangible brush of cobwebs across the face. There was no movement, anywhere. There was no one to move.

D'glas studied the field through narrowed eyes, but he could decipher no meaning from it. Not yet. The mystery was still as great as why the ships had suddenly stopped coming one hundred years ago.

The landing field had belonged to the colonies. The whole interplanetary enterprise had been theirs. The Hedonic Council, Earth's ruling body, had been content to leave it so, seeing no useful purpose in risking its concept of hedonism in a risky attempt to bring the colonists under control.

And to the Council's mind, no doubt, the colonies had served a useful purpose as places to which those few criminal masochists who rejected the ultimate sensual pleasure might exile themselves.

That was what Morgan had written in his book *The Rise and Fall of Applied Hedonics.*

What had happened, then, to the colonists who had worked the ships and run the field and operated the strip beyond?

D'glas frowned and went through the rusting ships nearby. When he emerged from the last of them, his frown was deeper.

Three of them had been unidentifiable. Of the remaining four, one was from Callisto, one from Ganymede, and two from Mars. Why they had come, why they had not left again, and what had happened to the crews were questions the ships did not answer.

D'glas turned toward the distant spires of the City. They rose like supplicating hands against the horizon, and he wished he were a complete hedonist. Perhaps then he could banish the tight, cold feeling of uneasiness that straightened his shoulders and stiffened his spine.

But he wasn't. He couldn't. He would have to live with it until he could answer the questions the silent City proposed.

It waited for him, motionless, deadly. . . .

Cautiously, he moved through the semidarkness of the building called Fun House, his senses alert. But there was nothing to set them off. No movement, no change, no sound.

Glass-doored booths lined both sides of the big room. They were empty. They were clean, too, dusted and scrubbed, the floors, the tables, the long, soft benches that were as wide as beds.

Idly he touched one of the dispensers that lined the wall above the table. White powder dusted from it and powdered the table top. He picked up a few grains on the tip of his finger and tasted them gingerly. They were sweet with an edge of bitterness. He studied the labels on the dispensers:

NEO-HEROIN POWDER
NEO-HEROIN SYRETTE
SCOTCH BOURBON GIN KAFI

He touched the last one: a hot drop of liquid fell onto his palm. He tasted it. It was bitter. Coffee, all right. Not good coffee, but coffee.

It was a puzzle. As far as his investigation had taken him, the strip was deserted. He had seen no signs of habitation, no activity, since he had entered the building through the underpass.

There was no one in this place. And yet it was ready for customers who might find here their definition of fun. It was clean. Dispensers were full. If he had coins to slip into the indicated slots, he could have had coffee or one of the other drinks listed.

It was all ready. Where was everybody?

He turned toward the rear of the room. From the outside this had looked like a multi-storied building. Even if all the levels were as tall as this one, there should be five more above. But he had found no way to reach them.

Then he found it. Where, logically, stairs should have started, where banks of elevators should have waited, there was a wall. Bolted in the middle of it was a metal plaque in archaic but decipherable printing:

DO NOT DISTURB
All Rooms Occupied
Sealed this day: 3–7–05

by order of the Council

D'glas puzzled over it. Occupied by what? Goods? People? Bodies?

All choices seemed improbable. He rapped on the plastic with his knuckles. It was solid and thick. Too solid and too thick to struggle with now. That mystery would have to wait.

As he approached the front of the building, doors swung open eerily. So all-pervasive had been the atmosphere of desertion, he almost jumped. Photosensitive relays and automatic motors, he told himself.

Beyond the entrance was a kind of arcade lined with machines. He studied them a moment. There were slots in them, obviously meant for coins. There were chutes from which something— possibly coins again—were returned. There they ceased to resemble each other. Some of the machines had handles, some levers, some no apparent means of control.

They were means, he decided, by which a person could wager coins against odds implicit in the machines or in the difficulties of controlling the gambler's own sensory or muscular system.

Coins, their use almost forgotten on Venus, seemed like very handy things to have on Earth. If he had a few, he might even return to that tap inside marked Kafi, whose dispensation, foul as it was, was still loaded with caffeine.

But wistful glances were a waste of time. He turned one of the machines around. Within five minutes he had solved the mystery of the rudimentary lock and picked it with the slender piece of wire which had kept half of his shirt-front neat and straight. Inside the machine, in a little box, were two lonely coins.

He juggled them thoughtfully in his hand, weighing the convenience of the coins against the effort necessary to obtain them, and turned to a second machine. Two coins were little better than none, but it wasn't necessary to spend time extracting them from the coin boxes. He had a stake.

In the second machine, steel balls, released simultaneously from right- and left-hand chutes, spiraled downward through mazes fraught with perils—holes through which they could drop and be lost. Electromagnets controlled by the player could guide the balls to safety and the jackpot at the bottom.

D'glas hit the jackpot with the first coin. Within ten minutes, he had milked every machine on that side of the arcade. None had many coins, but most had a few. As he turned away, he had a jacket pocket full of coins.

The games had been easy. Too easy. A ten-year-old child on Venus was expected to perform more difficult feats in his hedonic exercises.

Perhaps, he thought, they served as a come-on for the Fun House.

Thinking of the Fun House made him thirsty. He could suppress it, but there was no need now that he had coins.

The transparent doors opened to welcome him back. As they closed behind him, the lights went out.

The darkness was total. Suddenly, frighteningly, he was back in the coasting spaceship, feeling again that terrible, weightless disorientation—

Then his hedonic reflexes acted, damped the false sensory impressions, calmed his baseless fears. He knew, theoretically, what caused the darkness. An interrupter was canceling the light that should have reached him with waves 180° out of phase.

The darkness chuckled, snickered, giggled, tittered, guffawed, roared—

Suddenly, where only darkness had been, there was a fantastic figure standing in front of him—a creature who was goat from his wicked little hooves up to the waist, and man from the waist up to his curly hair. Out of the dark hair, like twin reminders, peeked sharp little horns.

"Be happy, be joyful, be gay!" bubbled the satyr. "Life begins at the Fun House of the Three Worlds, where every pleasure known to man has been brought to ecstatic perfection. What stimulation do your senses lack? Name it—and it's yours."

Stunned, his senses shocked, his body temporarily out of control, D'glas staggered back. Abruptly, the satyr disappeared, the laughter cut off in mid peal. Light returned, and D'glas realized that the darkness, the satyr, and the laughter had been only a recording, a welcome to the entering customer.

Where were the customers?

D'glas turned and walked quickly out of the arcade into the street beyond. He could explain the darkness inside the fun-house entrance; he could explain the laughter and the satyr. But he had an unreasonable reluctance to press through the darkness and the laughter, to brush past the satyr, to reach a fun house from which the fun had disappeared.

The naked sky had shaken him not long ago, but now it seemed preferable to the unnatural silence of a place that once had rocked with merriment. It was a place of strange echoes and unpleasant stillnesses.

He put it out of his mind. In front of him was a shop whose front wall was a single, broad sheet of glass. Across it was printed the word: FOODOMAT.

He walked along the front, looking for an entrance, and for a few steps he had a companion in the glass—a tall, lean, lonely young man gliding through a silent city.

A thin vertical line appeared in the glass, widened, became a door. D'glas hesitated in front of it, realized his hunger, and went in.

The floor was immaculate; the tables and benches were spotless. Glowing plastic railings guided him to the right. As he approached the side wall, delicate food odors stimulated involuntary flows of saliva into his mouth.

Set into the wall were plastic, full-color solidographs of prepared foods, some familiar, others strange. Below were names and coin slots. D'glas studied them:

CHLORELLA
Bread Loaf (hi-fat) Patty (lo-fat)
(Choose sauce below)

D'glas knew what chlorella was—a multipurpose omnifood on Venus. An alga whose fat and protein content could be adjusted to fit almost any requirement, it could be grown in vast quantities wherever sunlight (or its equivalent), carbon dioxide, water, and mineral salts were available. On Venus, it was grown in polyethylene tubing, nourished partially on recirculated human wastes; it not only fed the colonists, it renewed the oxygen supply.

Another food was strange.

PLANKTON
Cakes   Steak
Rare   Medium   Well done
(Choose sauce below)

Beyond were the synthetics: food fats from glycerin and petroleum, starches from the action of sunlight upon carbon monoxide, the amino acid proteins. D'glas knew these well.

He picked chlorella loaf, without sauce, and water. Chlorella was chlorella—there wasn't much anybody could do to it. Synthetics and sauces, on the other hand, were good things to steer clear of in a strange cuisine.

They always depended on the acquired tastes of the chemist and the cook.

The counter that ran along the wall opened up. The foods came through—the chlorella hot, the water cold. The dish and glass slid along the counter and waited for D'glas at the far end.

He carried them to the nearest table and tasted them gingerly. The water was pure within a fraction of one percent. The loaf was a good strain of chlorella ruined by poor seasoning; almost a teaspoon of salt and a dash of a sharp, unfamiliar condiment.

He ate quickly.

Satisfied but not sated, he stood up and walked toward the front of the large room. The glass opened for him, but he stopped, turned, and looked back. The empty dish and glass marred the neatness of the place. He restrained an irrational impulse to go back and remove them.

Who would care?

And who, he wondered, would come out when he was gone, to clear off the table and polish its top, to ready the restaurant for its next patron?

He suppressed a desire to call out, in the fashion of the childhood games played in the corridors and storerooms of the underground city called Morgantown. "Come out, come out, wherever you are!"

He shivered and went out into the warm, clear air, thinking that this life lived out-of-doors, without pressure suit or clouds or the endless rain, would take a long time to get used to.

The utter silence was oppressive. He stopped in the middle of the street, uncertain where to go next. The tallest building in sight had a sign that was even taller. MARS HOUSE.

D'glas walked quickly toward the red canopy. As he came under it, the walk moved beneath his feet. It was a slideway; it carried him to the portal and into the lobby.

As he stepped off, his feet gritted in red sand.

Overhead, invisibly suspended, was a sun looking oddly small. The sun might look like that when viewed from Mars.

The back wall was curved and shiny like the outer hull of a spaceship. The elevator installed against it was in an openwork frame, a replica of the portable models he had seen on the landing field.

"Joy!" said a voice at his elbow. "There are rooms available. May I help you?"

D'glas controlled an involuntary start and turned. He was standing beside a short desk. Above it was a mech consisting of two scanners and a speaker. One scanner studied the desk; the other, and the speaker, were pointed at D'glas. "I am the desk clerk," said the speaker. "How may I be of service?"

"What rooms are available?" D'glas asked slowly and distinctly.

"Only the second and third floors, sir. The other thirty floors are filled. The rooms we have left, however, are fully equipped for temporary or permanent residence. Just slip your IDisk beneath my scanner—"

"What do you mean—permanent residence?" D'glas interrupted, at the risk of jamming the mech beyond usefulness.

"Ah, there you are, M'Gregor!" a strange voice broke in. "We've been looking for you."

D'glas spun around.

Close behind him, a smile on his craggy face, was a man D'glas had never seen before.

III

That action is best which procures the greatest happiness for the greatest numbers.

FRANCIS HUTCHESON

"Sorry to startle you," said the stranger, with an engaging grin. "To tell the truth, we couldn't resist seeing your reaction to someone's voice when you thought you were in a deserted city."

It was a likable demonstration of humanity, but it brought up more questions than it answered. "Who is 'we'?" D'glas asked evenly.

The stranger grimaced. "Sorry again. That's the royal 'we,' I'm afraid. The name is Hansen." He stuck out a strong, square hand, its back furry with curly, blond hair.

D'glas took it. It felt hard, warm, and dry. "How did you know what I thought?" he asked, studying Hansen. He was as tall as D'glas and broader across the shoulders. He seemed about ten years older.

Hansen's eyebrows, almost white against his tanned face, moved expressively. "Rather obvious," he said easily. "Not much else a man can think about the City. Because it's almost true."

D'glas hesitated. There were so many questions to ask that he had difficulty choosing the next. And Hansen's answers were peculiarly unsatisfactory.

"Look!" Hansen said apologetically. "You want to know a mess of things—what's happened to the City, how I happen to know your name, where everybody is, and so on. Let's mosey over to the Council building, where we can be comfortable, and the Council will tell you everything you want to know. Okay?"

"It's not okay," D'glas said dryly, "but I guess it will have to do."

"Cigarette?" Hansen extended a metal case filled with stuffed paper cylinders. "But no—you wouldn't have picked up the habit on Venus, would you? No oxygen to spare, right? These, though, are rather special—a blend of synthetic alkaloids that supply a wonderful lift without danger of lung irritation. Don't want to short the lifespan with carcinogens, eh? Habit-forming as neo-heroin, though." He put one between his lips and sucked on it. The tip glowed and began to burn; smoke curled from his nose. "Shall we go?"

"Just a moment. I was about to get a straightforward answer to a straightforward question from this mech."

"Touché!" Hansen laughed. "But that's a simple mech. I'm afraid the answer you get will be just as unsatisfying."

"What do you mean by permanent residence?" D'glas repeated.

"Permanent residence," said the clerk mechanically, "is permanent residence."

Hansen slapped D'glas on the shoulders. "See? This mech was built to accept registrations, not to explain itself. That's something even we would have difficulty with, eh?"

"Perhaps," D'glas admitted.

As Hansen stepped onto the slideway, it reversed itself and carried him toward the street.

Watchfully, D'glas followed.

"This way," Hansen said cheerfully. He walked to the nearest corner, turned, and started down broad, worn marble steps under glowing letters that said: J.R.T. DOWNTOWN.

Hansen dropped coins into a turnstile and pushed through.

"You still pay?" D'glas asked when he had rejoined him.

"Absolutely. Be immoral not to, eh? Can't let standards slip when society is depending on you." He hopped onto an escalator that took them down to a broad platform bordered by slideways. "This way," he said gayly, hopping nimbly to the left.

D'glas followed, feeling more at home underground, fighting a delusion of safety.

The slideway paralleled an endless parade of small, two-passenger, moving cars with one seat facing the front. Hansen stepped into one. D'glas sat down beside him.

"Everything still works," D'glas said. "Food ready, drinks on tap, transportation system running. Everything ready. And nobody to—"

"Yeah," Hansen agreed, cocking a pale eyebrow. "Pitiful, isn't it? Faithful old automaton keeping things all ready for the masters who have gone away. Old Mech Tray; that sort of thing."

"Or as if someone had gone off and left the water running," D'glas suggested.

"That, too. Better fasten your safety belt."

Hansen was already strapping himself down. Glancing once at the smooth, glowing tunnel walls, D'glas shrugged and tightened the belt across his legs. The cars were moving at the less-than-dangerous speed of 100 kilometers an hour. Being linked together, they could move no faster unless the whole, endless chain speeded up.

"Drink?" Hansen asked, indicating the dispensers lining the front of the car. "All the ethyloids. Synthetic, of course, but then, what isn't? Or maybe you'd like a shot of neo-heroin. That would bring the world into focus."

"Thanks," D'glas said dryly. "I prefer my own focus. Your comments seem to agree with my assumption that there are no more people around."

"That's right," Hansen agreed. "They do, don't they? But that isn't quite accurate. They're around—just not *around*. If you know what I mean."

D'glas resisted an urge to smash Hansen's amused smile down his irritating throat. "And everything continues automatically, is that it?"

"Right. It follows, doesn't it? Labor is unpleasant. Unpleasure is illegal. Labor is illegal. *Q.E.D.* Therefore, everything is automatic."

D'glas nodded slowly. The advantages were obvious, the disadvantages not so readily apparent. At the sacrifice of immediate progress, the colonists could mechanize Morgantown and the other settlements, could equip the combines with automatic pilots. And then—He considered the prospect. What then?

"And then," Hansen continued with inexorable logic, "everyone can devote himself to pleasure—which is, after all, the only good, eh? And the millennium is at hand—pure hedonism. Let joy reign unconfined! And speaking of joy, boy, hold your hat. Here we go again!"

From the brilliance of the glowing tunnel walls, the car dived unexpectedly into the darkness of an interrupter. *Dived* was the proper word. D'glas felt himself rise from his seat as the car plunged downward; then he was slammed down hard as the car hit bottom and straightened out. Or perhaps it started upward again. Everything was happening so fast that D'glas's perceptions became confused.

Perched on the front of the car, talons disappearing into the hard metal, was an alien horror fluorescing greenly. From the waist up, it was woman—except for the wings, and they belonged with the feathered half, below.

It opened green lips. "Welcome, mortal," it drawled. "You've kept me waiting long enough!"

"Don't mind her," whispered a voice in D'glas's right ear, the one away from Hansen. "She's always impatient. She's a harpy, you know."

Before D'glas could turn his head to see who was whispering, a second winged thing appeared beside the harpy. This one was purple, also female, with snaky hair that weaved as if it had a life of its own. If possible, her face was more horrid than the harpy's.

"Move on, sister," it snarled to the harpy in a deep voice. "He's mine. After all, he has sinned."

"Haven't we all?" snapped the harpy. "You can have him when I get through, dearie. You've been satisfied with my leavings before."

"The purple one's a Fury," the voice whispered in his ear. "Don't pay any attention to them. They're mad. They're women, you know."

Out of the darkness in front, the blue, three-headed dog sprang between the woman-things, its serpent tail lashing, its three jaws agape and dripping. It sprang straight for D'glas's throat.

"Don't flinch," the voice whispered hurriedly. "They can't hurt you. They aren't in your cultural heritage at all."

Cerberus, the dog, hurtled through D'glas's body and disappeared. He was braced for the impact and felt foolish when there was none.

It was illusion, D'glas knew—but real enough. Too real. He did not like the implications at all.

This time he would look at the thing that whispered on his shoulder, he decided, but something stopped him again. The harpy and the Fury had disappeared. In their place was a horned, tailed creature attired in fluorescent red scales; in one hand he carried a pitchfork, in the other, casually, his spiked tail.

"Well, M'Gregor," he rolled out with great sophistication and an urbane, man-to-man smile, "we meet at last. I'll bet you thought you'd ditched me for good back there in the Middle Ages. But there's no escaping the consciousness of sin, is there? Of course not. I've always considered myself the kind of creature who, if he had not existed, would have had to have been invented.

"Where there is sin, there is hell, whether we put it off to the Hereafter or make it now ourselves. To know sin is to feel guilt, to feel guilt is to be punished. The only limiting factor on the punishment is the limits of our own imaginations. I'm sure we can agree on these things, eh? Come, little ones, let us show our friend what we are talking about."

They swarmed over the front of the car, the little demons, wielding spears, pitchforks, swords, knives, needles, stabbers of all kinds. Pain started in D'glas's foot, traveled up his calf, tormented his thigh, reached his hips, climbed to his abdomen, reached for his heart—

The car plunged into a red inferno, a pit of molten lava. Heat poured over the car, over D'glas, fantastically, intolerably. D'glas lifted from his seat as the car dived straight into the middle of it.

"Mephistopheles, eh?" the voice chuckled in his ear. "Anachronous psychiatry is what I call it. Freud with hellfire."

The scaly thing and its spawn were gone. In the car ahead was an impossibly ugly crone, almost toothless, dressed in filthy rags. She was stirring a pot and dropping indescribable substances into it; nameless things swooped around her head. She looked up, saw D'glas, and cackled.

"A handsome lad. I knew you'd come. He promised me. A young man, strong in the loins, He said, just for me. Oh, we'll be happy together, we two, like a pair of doves. We'll do our devotions together—the kind He likes. When the Coven meets, why we'll be there to share the fun, and you'll be my partner in the orgy. Oh, we'll worship the Goat, we will." She cackled again. "All will be afeard of us and pay us tribute, night or day, for the things that we might do: the curse, the evil, the witch's brew. Oh, we'll have fun, lovey, you and I."

The dark, nameless things circled closer to D'glas's head. He could not control a shudder.

The crone squinted one eye knowingly. "I don't look too pretty now, but wait till you've sampled what's in my kettle. Then you'll see me with different eyes. To you I'll be young again, straight-bodied, firm-fleshed, and curved like a girl should be. You'll love me then, my boy. You'll never leave my side; you'll never get enough of touching me."

She lifted a spoon out of the pot and tasted the brew gingerly, one eye squinting judiciously. Lips smacking, she nodded her approval and dipped in the spoon again. This time she held it high with a bony hand and put one leg over the car which held Hansen and D'glas.

"Now it's your turn, lad," she crooned. "Open your ruby lips, lovey, and soon the world will be a different place for you and me —a place of light in the darkness and darkness in the light. Come now, lad!" She had both legs over. She was close, the spoon dripping. "Open up!"

D'glas didn't move.

"That's right," the voice whispered approvingly in his ear. "Not your dish at all."

The spoon passed through D'glas's face, and the crone disappeared, her face twisted with disappointment.

"I'm your dish," the thing on his shoulder whispered. "Or maybe you're my dish. It doesn't matter really. We were meant for each other."

This time D'glas got his head turned. Sitting on his right shoulder was an inky blob. It was nothingness personified. It was unconsciousness. It was surrender. It was the merging of the individual will into the collective will, the betrayal of all personal standards, the collectivization of the psyche.

It was everything D'glas hated. It was the reverse side of the hedonic coin, the sin to match hedonism's virtue, the hell to balance its heaven.

Only these were words, and words are meaningless in anything except a personal sense. In all heavens there is the germ of hell; in all hells, of heaven.

The blob opened bright, blue eyes and a pink mouth. "There, now," it whispered. "Aren't you glad you waited?"

It melted toward him, blurring, filtering through the skin and bones into his skull in an unholy symbiosis. Mutely, D'glas struggled against the intolerable invasion.

Light burst into the darkness, shattered it, sent it fleeing. For a moment D'glas was blind. Then sight returned.

The car was poised on an incredible summit. The sun blazed down on them. The spires of tall buildings were so far below they looked like spikes waiting to impale them. Thousands of meters in the air, they hung between sky and earth, exposed to the perils of each.

In spite of his training, D'glas's heart thundered in his chest.

The car just ahead toppled over the peak, pulling D'glas's car to the edge. It hesitated on the brink of a precipice.

The car dropped, fell, dived, plunged, plummeted. It was worse than the weightlessness that followed the cut-out of the rocket drive on the trip from Venus. They screamed down the side of the cliff into the endless depths below, waiting for them, dark and shadowed.

D'glas gripped the side of the car with desperate hands, feeling himself lifted from his seat, flung outward. It went on and on, the spires of the buildings rising to meet them, flashing past, the windows blurred on either side. And finally came the sickening onset of weight again as the car hit bottom and leveled off in the glowing tunnel once more and rolled peacefully forward as if there had been nothing really to be frightened of.

Hansen was standing. "Here we are," he said cheerily. "Coming?"

He hopped onto the slideway that ran beside the car. For a moment D'glas hesitated. Taking a deep breath, he unsnapped his safety belt and joined Hansen as he moved from highspeed to lowspeed and then to a platform that was motionless.

Ahead was an escalator that took them to the foot of stairs that mounted into the open air. Hansen paused to let D'glas catch up. He grinned. "Like the joy ride?"

"Joy ride?" D'glas echoed grimly. "That's what you call it?"

"Some people like to be frightened, you know. It gives them the sense of being alive, stimulates their adrenals, tones up their whole system. Mostly they aren't—alive, that is. Not in any meaningful sense. They exist at a minimum level. If they can achieve the exhilaration of danger while clinging to a subconscious realization that they are completely protected, they have gained worlds without expense."

"Thanks. I'll stimulate my own adrenals," D'glas said dryly. "When anyone wanted to go anywhere else in the city, he had to go through that?"

"Oh, no. That would scarcely be hedonism, would it? When this City was really humming, there were helijets and surface cars and buses until the sky and streets were black. And less eventful subways." Hansen smiled broadly. "But, as you reminded me, that was all in the past. All things considered, it was an inefficient, wasteful method of procuring a really simple result: pleasure. And so it is only a relic."

"And yet, like everything else, it keeps running?"

"Necessarily." Hansen winked. "You noticed the apparitions, I imagine. Symbols all, as you realized. Sort of a basic subconscious-to-subconscious hookup, eh? Well, I won't bore you with an interpretation which would, necessarily, be faulty. But did you notice that they were all personifications of sin and its psychological concomitant, guilt?"

D'glas was silent. He studied the blank-eyed buildings on either side of the darkening, twilit canyons through which they walked; the spires were gravestones in a vast necropolis, the burial ground of man's hopes of conquest and dreams of peace. They hid, as well, a mystery within them or beneath them: *how? why?* It was a mystery he had to solve, for in it lay the answer to a basic question about mankind and its future.

Wherever he was, on Earth or Venus, on Mars or Ganymede or Callisto, whatever refinements were grafted upon him, man was man, prey to the same fears, nurse to the same hopes and dreams.

Ahead, like sunlight breaking through the banks of clouds to spotlight an unexpected realization or a sudden truth, an opening in the canyon wall let in brightness and a promise of something new and vital.

"You did, of course," Hansen continued without waiting for an answer. "You are a thoughtful, perceptive person. Sin and guilt.

You would think that they would be outlawed from a hedonic world. In a sense, you would be right. Yet you would be overlooking something—the pleasures of the illicit, for without prohibition there is no pleasure; there is only contentment and the satisfaction of minor animal desires. Without hell, there is no heaven.

"And, to provide the ultimate in criminal thrill, there was that most illicit of all sensations—pain. For without pain, there is no ecstasy; there is only insensibility."

"I am not concerned with ecstasy," D'glas said sharply. "Where are we going?"

"As I told you: to the Council!"

"Where all my questions will be answered," D'glas finished, dryly. "That's fine. But where is the Council?"

"Ahead. Don't be impatient. That is unpleasure, and unpleasure is a crime."

"Then there is no pleasure. Riddle me no more paradoxes, Hansen," D'glas said firmly. "Point it out!"

Hansen pointed a blunt forefinger. "There. The tallest building of that group. There is the Council."

The building was like orange flame against opaque blueness, reflecting the setting sun. It was walled in metal, a flame flattened at the top. It was perhaps four blocks away and one over. There were taller buildings in other areas but none as spectacular.

D'glas didn't like the looks of it.

The canyon walls had broken around them. To the right a wide, paved walk cut through green lawn toward a low, massive building. The grass made D'glas feel warm again. It was the first real *life* he had seen since landing. Someone had taken care of it, mowed, it, tended it, kept it green. Not a mech, because there were imperfections—a bareness here and there, a clump of grass uneven.

It reminded him of Venus. Only here the process had been reversed: Man had been busy turning fertile soil into a vast, stony desert.

The building was decaying. Much of the façade had fallen; it lay in heaps of rubble along the steps and across the entranceway. Only this building and the landing field had not been kept in repair.

"What is the Council?" he asked.

"The Council?" Hansen began. "Why, the Council—"

Seconds before, D'glas had seen the flicker of movement beside the building. Now he heard the stone whistle through the air; it struck with a hollow, thumping sound.

Hansen collapsed slowly, his head laid open to the split metal beneath. Inside his skull, tiny wires glistened.

The thing hit the pavement and lay still.

IV

So act as to treat humanity, whether in your own person or in another, always as an end, and never as only a means.

IMMANUEL KANT

D'glas spun back toward the building, suppressing his irritation. The Hansen-mech was out of commission, at least temporarily. He had to decide, and quickly, whether his best opportunity lay here on the pavement or waited there beside the building.

He might discover something from a dissection of the mech, but the chances were against it. Someone was standing on a heap of rubble, tiptoeing tall to see what lay on the pavement beside him, and his decision was made.

The stone-thrower was a girl.

He sprinted toward the building. As he ran, he analyzed her. Her position on the rubble made her seem taller than she was. She was less than two meters tall, a small, slender, dark-haired girl with an oval face and blue eyes that widened now as they saw how swiftly he was approaching.

She stood for a moment, poised, her right hand ready to throw the rock it held, and then she turned, leaping from the mound, and ran swiftly around the corner of the building. D'glas raced after her.

He was just in time to see her dive through a small side doorway. At the door, he pulled up, half expecting it to be locked. But the metal door swung toward him as he tugged at it; it squealed, protesting, but it opened. Within was darkness. He entered cautiously, went down a short flight of steps, and walked into crowded shadows.

As his eyes adjusted to the shadows, he realized what the shadows were, and he recognized the function of the building. The shadows were cases; the cases were filled with books; the building was a library. The air was filled with the dry, tickling odor of dust and decay.

He was running now, thinking of the wealth of knowledge in this room alone. There were few books on Venus, a treasure or two smuggled from Earth before the ships stopped coming. The rest of their inheritance from the past was on microfilm and could have been stored in its entirety in a room much smaller than this. Even new books were on microfilm; plastics were far easier to make than paper, and underground space is always a problem. Perhaps some day Venus would return to the relatively simpler art of making paper and books, when trees were more useful for making pulp than for making oxygen.

But the question was: had the girl stopped to hide or had she kept running?

D'glas stopped abruptly, and heard the sound of running feet, fading in the distance. He sprinted again.

He went through a doorway and up long, wide stairs to a broad, tall lobby; it was bigger than anything he had seen within walls. But there was no time to react. Shoes pounded above him, the corner of a blue skirt swirled, and there were more stairs to climb. He ran, his legs flashing, devouring the steps, and yet the girl kept ahead.

There was a third flight of stairs, and then the girl ran toward the rear of the building, through a doorway from which wooden doors had rotted and dropped away. Again they ran between stacks, countless rows of them, holding books by the thousands, by the millions.

Still D'glas could not catch up.

Surely, he thought, there will be a place where she can run no farther.

There were more stairs, but this time they were narrow metal ones with rusty iron bars for treads. Every few steps one of them sagged under D'glas's weight. Rust scaled away in a continuous rain, below him and above.

And at last the end came. At the top of the last flight of metal steps, the girl stood on a narrow landing, tugging futilely at a metal door through which orange sunlight streamed dustily.

D'glas started up the stairs. The girl spun. Her arm flashed back. The rock was ready in it. "Stay where you are!" she said, her bosom rising and falling only a little faster than normal. "You'll get what the other got."

She had a pleasant voice. Even uttering threats, it was low and feminine. "My reflexes are better than the mech's," D'glas panted. "I'll catch the rock, and then where will you be?" He climbed another step; the whole flight sagged under him.

"Don't be ridiculous!" she snapped, her eyes furiously blue. "Back!" Her arm tensed.

D'glas jumped to the floor, his eyes flicking briefly to the old, iron stanchion that supported the corner of the landing on which the girl stood. Perhaps the door above leaked. Whatever the reason the bar was rotten with rust; in one spot, it was eaten almost in two. His weight had buckled it outward, but now it held again.

D'glas moved over beside the landing and looked up. "Why can't we be friends?"

"What's that?" she asked bitterly. "Only people can be friends."

"Well?" he asked, puzzled. Then his face cleared. "Oh, and you're not?"

"Don't taunt me!" she warned, her arm tensed again.

"I see. You think I'm not people."

"Of course you're not! I'm the only one left in the city; perhaps the only one in the world. It's just another of the Council's tricks."

"I don't know what you mean by that, but if you're the only one left you should be glad to see me." D'glas grinned. "I'm from Venus."

Her arm hesitated and then readied itself again. "I don't believe you. You were with the mech."

"Why not? It was taking me to the Council."

"Why should you want to go to the Council?"

"To find out what's happened here. To tell the Council what's happened on Venus. To ask for help. As a matter of fact, your missile came at an inopportune moment. It was obvious from the start that it wasn't human. With that advantage, I hoped to accomplish something."

"Don't live on illusions!"

He liked this girl, her appearance, her independence, her quick mind. "But how did you know it wasn't human?" he asked abruptly.

She laughed without mirth. "After so long, you can sense them —the little imperfection in the way they walk, their hidden reservoir of power, their single-mindedness. But then, what else could it be? I told you I was the only one left."

"If you can sense them, you should be able to sense that I'm not one of them," D'glas pointed out gently.

She frowned thoughtfully. "They've tried to trick me before, but it's the first time I've been chased. Maybe I think you're what you pretend to be. But I can't take chances. What proof do I have?"

"What proof have I," D'glas said slowly, "that *you're* human?"

Slowly, thoughtfully, her arm lowered. Instantly, D'glas lunged into the rusted stanchion. It snapped. The landing sagged with an animal screech of bolts dragged from the wall.

At the first movement, the girl whirled, reaching for the doorknob, but the landing sagged a little more, throwing her against the railing. She leaped. The landing toppled beneath her, rending its way downward.

Her hands clawed at the door and missed. She fell backward toward the floor and twisted metal that had preceded her.

Miraculously dodging the falling stairway, D'glas was waiting for her. His arms scooped her out of the air. He caught her right hand immediately, but the rock was gone.

For a moment, gasping, she let herself crumple against him. After the first impact, she wasn't heavy. She was, he realized with some surprise, quite an interesting armful. It was not entirely because she was the first girl he had seen in three months. The first human, in fact, he corrected quickly—but it was the feminity that made it interesting.

"There," he said gayly, smiling into her drawn face, "that's better, isn't it?"

Her color flooded back, and one fist fetched him a stinging clout along the jaw. He dropped her.

She landed in the wreckage of the stairs. She stiffened. "Owwww!" she cried out, and scrambled up quickly with a sound of ripping plastic, rubbing the injured area. Almost speechless with anger, she spluttered, "You— You—"

D'glas touched his jaw and waggled it experimentally to see if it was broken. He decided that it wasn't. "You didn't seem to appreciate my rescuing you," he said innocently.

Her face worked for a moment. She sniffled. A sob broke from her throat. Two tears gathered in the corners of her eyes, tore free, and coursed muddy channels through the dust on her face. She began to cry.

D'glas was shocked. He had not seen tears since he had been a child. Now they left him helpless.

Understanding came. She was only a girl, a young one, and

alone. She had put up a good fight against a man who had been hedonically trained and tested in competition. Defeated, hurt, humiliated, defenseless, it was little wonder that she sobbed.

Gently he took her in his arms; he pulled her close. She came, unresisting, weeping. She cried against the shoulder. "There, there," he said ineffectually, patting her clumsily on the back. "That's all right. I'm sorry."

Slowly the sobs turned to sniffles and the sniffles to uneven breaths that caught in her throat. As she regained self-control, she drew back, wiping the tears away with the back of one hand. It left black smudges across her cheeks.

She was a little girl, he thought tenderly. An urchin. She had been playing with the big boys and got hurt. He caught her shoulder and tried to turn her around. "Are you hurt bad?" he asked solicitously.

She pulled herself away and put one hand behind her. "Never mind!" she said with great dignity. "It's nothing."

D'glas shrugged, his fatherly instincts submerged before her sudden return to maturity. He watched her closely.

"Well," she said defiantly, "what now?"

He smiled, liking her. "Now, some answers."

"What makes you think you'll get them?"

"I'll get them," he said confidently. "But there must be a better place than this to talk. Lead me to it!" She hesitated. "Please?" he added.

She shrugged, as if recognizing the futility of resistance, and moved away among the stacks, one hand behind to hold together her torn skirt. D'glas stayed close to her, watchful for the smallest sign that she was going to break away.

"I'm D'glas M'Gregor," he said. "And I still want to be friends."

For a moment her back remained stiff. Then, over her shoulder, she said, "Susan."

"Susan what?"

"Just Susan. When there's only one person left—or two or three—there's no need for more names than one."

"Then you've been alone for a long time."

"Since I was ten. That's when my mother died. She died in childbirth, refusing the Council's help. My father assisted, but nothing could have saved her. The son they wanted died too. A few weeks later I lost Father."

"How?"

She gave him a quick glance over her shoulder. "He was unhappy. He couldn't fight it. He never got over my mother's death. So the Council took him."

"He's dead, then?"

"No. Just gone. Like the others. Since then I've been alone. Ten years alone." Her shoulders straightened, as if to repress a shiver.

"That's over now," D'glas said kindly. "You don't have to be alone any more."

As they came to the broad staircase, she let him draw even with her, and the glance she gave him was almost friendly. Immediately, she looked away. He resisted an impulse to touch her. It wasn't time. But it was pleasant, anticipating.

On the second floor, she led him to a door inset with translucent glass. Across it was printed: HEAD LIBRARIAN.

Beyond it was a living room furnished and decorated with excellent taste; yet it did not sacrifice comfort. It was a room he liked instantly. Even his highly trained sensory discriminations could find no flaw in it.

Beyond, through a hall, was a bedroom, just as tastefully planned and arranged but more feminine. Between the rooms, off the hall, was a necessary.

"If you don't mind," Susan said with heavy irony, "I'd like to clean up and change my clothes."

"Certainly," Douglas said. But he kept her under observation as he moved into the bedroom and went quickly through the drawers that slid out of the wall at his touch. They held clothing only—fresh, never-worn synthetics. There were two closets. Behind one sliding door were dresses and suits. A floor rack, swinging out, was stacked with shoes.

Behind the second door was an armory.

D'glas had never seen a real weapon before, but he called on his memory, reviewing an almost forgotten strip.

There were minims, tiny hand guns; machine pistols; high-velocity rifles with explosive bullets; a rocket launcher; racks of grenades—

D'glas slid the door shut and turned to Susan. "Sorry I can't trust you yet," he apologized, "but I can't afford to let you run away because you're frightened, or kill me because you don't understand. My mission is too important. Pick out what clothing you want. Bring it with you."

He watched her as she selected it, ignoring her displeasure. When she had her arms filled, he led the way to the necessary. It was more ample than most, but the equipment, except for a small dressing table in one corner, was standard. The cubicle was windowless. The only exit, except for the door, was the disposal chute, and that was too narrow even for Susan's slimness.

As he left the room, Susan demanded petulantly, "What's so important about your mission? If you really are from Venus, what do you want with the Council? What did you want to tell the Council?"

"We're being observed by aliens," D'glas said. "Their purpose —" he shrugged—"we can only guess at. Probably conquest."

The necessary door slid shut. The last sentence he had to say softly to himself.

"But it looks as if they beat me here."

D'glas waited patiently. It was half an hour before Susan emerged, scrubbed, her face glowing with subcutaneous health, her hair damp and curly from the shower's steam. She was wearing a loose-fitting gray suit, her hand resting casually in one pocket of the jacket, seemingly careless of the effect her appearance had on him.

But it was only seeming. No woman spends half an hour merely getting clean; no woman picks out clothing that compliments her appearance and coloring so much as this gray suit flattered Susan; no woman applies cosmetics so carefully that they are undetectable—unless she is concerned about some man's opinion.

"Beautiful!" D'glas said. "But you know that."

She shook her head. "I didn't know it." But her eyes were wide, and he had a distant understanding, suddenly, what it must be like to grow up alone. It was surprising she was so normal.

"Sit down," he said, patting the love seat cushion beside him. She sat down gingerly. "Your father must have been a hedonist," he said.

She nodded. "That's right. The last of the real hedonists. You know what a hedonist is?"

D'glas smiled tolerantly. "On Venus we have what they tried to build here—a society founded on basic hedonic principles. A careful balance between objective reality and subjective attitude."

Her eyes shone. "That must be heaven," she whispered.

"I don't see how it could be improved," D'glas admitted, and paused, wondering. A few months ago, he hadn't considered it so perfect. But then there had been nothing with which to compare it. Perhaps the Hansen-mech was right: in order to appreciate heaven, one must have hell. "And yet," he added honestly, "there's hard work; no end of that. The joy of bringing a dead planet to life is never done. But, of course, everything depends on the attitude."

"Certainly. I know hedonics. My father taught me, before he left. After that I kept up the studies and the exercises which taught me that as long as I was happy, I was safe from the Council. My freedom depended on it."

She was slowly relaxing. Her back had touched the backrest of the love seat.

"You lived here—the three of you—until your mother died. And then, because your father was grieved by your mother's death, the Council took him." She nodded. "Why?" he asked. "I don't understand."

"It was against the law," she said, frowning. "To be unhappy, that is. We were safe as long as we were happy, and we were happy, for ten years. The only three people left in the world, happy together. Strictly speaking, Father shouldn't have let himself become emotionally involved with us and, in a way, that was his tragedy. The Inconstancy clause of the Hedonic Oath bound him not to love or wed or father; then he could always perform his duties to his dependents. But we were his only dependents, and he thought he was safe."

"Since then you've lived here all alone," D'glas said softly, his voice and face sympathetic. "Poor kid."

She bit her lower lip because it had begun to tremble. "It wasn't so bad," she said bravely. "The worst was realizing that Father loved Mother more than he loved me. Oh, I realized later how silly that was. And then trying to be happy even though they both were gone. But I had to, because I knew how important it was."

D'glas put his hand protectively over hers. She let it stay there. "Funny," he mused. "Everything else is maintained. Only the landing field and this library have been allowed to deteriorate. Why?"

"There was no more use for the field. Why should anyone want to leave when he could have happiness here—couldn't escape it, in fact? His wanting to leave was prima facie evidence of unhappiness and made him a criminal, subject to sentence."

"Sentence?" D'glas echoed.

Her fingers tightened on his. "Sentenced to paradise. The library was in the same category. What was the point in preserving it? Knowledge was only a means, and it had done all it could;

paradise was available. Knowledge, in itself, never made anyone happy. Progress could go no farther. There is nothing beyond perfection, and paradise is perfection, by definition. So we could live here—we three refugees from paradise—as long as we were happy." Her voice trembled. "But we weren't satisfied. Desire entered, and with it came discontent, change, death, sorrow—"

Her voice broke. She turned toward D'glas blindly, her face seeking. He welcomed her into his arms; his lips descended to her, gently at first and then more firmly. She melted against him.

She moved in his arms. Something small and hard pressed into his abdomen. "That's enough," she said coldly.

D'glas glanced down. In her right hand was a minim, its barrel trying to leave its imprint on his body "Where did you get that?" he asked in amazement.

"I keep one clipped inside the disposal chute in case I'm ever surprised in the necessary," she said without inflection. "Get up!" D'glas stood up. "Walk toward the door, slowly." D'glas obeyed. "Open it. Take one step forward and turn around. Don't make any sudden moves. I'll shoot at your shadow. Now close the door."

D'glas frowned at the translucent glass panel and the words printed on it: HEAD LIBRARIAN. Was she mad? And then he realized that she was not; she was just careful. The glass panel doubled as a fluorescent screen. He was being X-rayed.

He relaxed, and his mind drifted to what she had said about her father—gone but not dead. When she flung open the door, he said, "Susan. The Council—"

"D'glas!" she cried, unheeding. "You *are* human! I was afraid to believe it, afraid that—" And then her lips found his, clumsy at first but infinitely educable and learning fast, and the time for questions was past. . . .

D'glas raised himself on one elbow, "Susan," he began, "you were going to tell me—" He stopped. She was asleep, her cheeks flushed, her hair like a dark, soft halo on the pillow beneath her head, beautiful beyond description.

He smiled ruefully. Every time he was about to learn something about this crazy world, there was an interruption.

V

And there is even a happiness
That makes the heart afraid.
THOMAS HOOD

D'glas awoke instantly, feeling alone and apprehensive. Beside him, the bed was empty. He touched the sheet. Cold. "Susan!" he called.

Sooner than the silence, the echoes told him that Susan was gone. Except for him, the rooms were empty.

Against the drapes that covered the tall windows, the morning sun was beating. A pale imitation of its brilliance filtered through to him.

So truth, he thought dismally, filters through the barrier of our senses.

He sat up, hugging his knees, and faced the fact of his insufficiency. He was not master of himself and his happiness as he had thought. Unsuspecting, he had surrendered his hedonic state to an outsider, a girl with blue eyes to see him as he was, with soft lips to lure him, with dark hair to wind around his heart.

Against his will, he was in love with Susan.

It was not part of the plan. It could be disastrous.

From the available evidence, the aliens had already conquered Earth. Where the humans were, if they were still alive, was uncertain, although by now D'glas could make a shrewd guess.

The inescapable fact: he was one man—hedonically trained though he was—pitted against vast and undefined forces. It was an unfortunate time to lose effective control over his ductless glands and their dangerous secretions.

Even now, at the unsought memory of Susan—her courage, her independence, her beauty, her firm body, her need of him— he felt a soft outpouring of affection, his adrenals, his pituitaries, his hypothalamus working automatically.

The thought that he might have lost her, that somehow, by some tragic circumstance, she might never return to him, made him weak and sapped his powers of movement and decision. He frowned savagely and refused to think of Susan in any personal sense. With an effort born of desperation, he succeeded in thinking of her only as an auxiliary to his main purpose.

This was certain: his duty came first.

He slipped out of bed. A few minutes in the necessary cleansed him, refreshed him, depilated his day-old beard. Emerging, he considered with distaste the prospect of resuming the clothing he had worn yesterday, but there was no help for it. Susan's clothing was not only the wrong shape; it was much too small.

He shrugged, reflecting: What cannot be cured must be endured. Dressed, he inspected the clothes closet. Only a pair of shorts and a tunic were missing.

A minim and several grenades were gone from the armory. The grenades were about twice the size of his thumb nail. They were armed by flipping over a lever against the tug of a spring. When the lever was released, it sprang back. There was probably a few seconds after that before explosion. D'glas slipped a handful into one jacket pocket.

He took a machine pistol and broke it down. Its method of operation was simple, and it was in good shape, the parts clean and glistening with a thin film of oil. He snapped it back together and put it in the other pocket.

The magazine held fifty bullets which could be fired singly or in bursts of five. He wouldn't need any more ammunition. Open warfare—one man against a world—would be insane.

His eyes were alert as he left the bedroom, but they noticed nothing out of place until he reached the door. Fastened to the glass was a sheet of paper. On it was handwriting, the spelling archaic, the phrasing quaint, but the writing slender, well-formed, and attractive—like Susan herself:

You looked tired, so I did not wake you. I have gone out for food and clothing. It was improvident of me, I suppose, not to have these things on hand, but I did not expect to have a man around.

D'glas smiled involuntarily and then turned it into a frown. He read on:

Don't be alarmed if I'm not here when you wake up, or if I'm delayed in returning. There is small danger in this kind of foraging and I am used to it. Don't worry. I have survived alone for ten years. I write survived because I do not count the days before yesterday as living.

Wait for me, darling. I love you.

SUSAN

D'glas studied the note expressionlessly. Then he picked up the mechanical pen from the table beside the door and wrote, beneath Susan's signature:

Couldn't wait. After this is over, I'll return if I can. Stay here. Don't get involved.

He frowned at it. It was, perhaps, more brusque than he had intended, but he resisted the impulse to soften it with sentiment. Sentiment was dangerous. Until his mission was completed, one way or another, he had to stay away from Susan, he had to fight free of the emotional entanglements that could only spell disaster.

He tossed the pen down with unintended vigor and walked

quickly, impatiently, out of the room and down the broad steps to the library entrance.

The Hansen-mech was still lying on the sidewalk. There was one significant change. The neck was an empty stalk; where the head had been, there was a black spot on the pavement. Scattered across the sidewalk were fragments of metal and something that resembled sponge platinum.

Deadly little Susan, D'glas thought.

Something snuffled.

D'glas looked up quickly. Coming toward him, filling the street from side to side, flanked by two miniature editions of itself, came a swishing, snuffling monster.

It was only fifty meters away.

D'glas leaped, turned, raced for the shelter of the library, and swung back toward the street, the machine pistol ready in his right hand, a grenade in the other. And he felt foolish.

The monster was a streetcleaner mech. Its gaping mouth reached from curb to curb, snuffling up dust and refuse. Underneath its flat, slick body, particles danced as ultrasonic vibrations loosened stubborn dirt and grease and whisked them away. Behind it, the street gleamed like polished metal.

The smaller mechs cleaned the sidewalks. All three of the automatic machines ignored him.

As he watched, the nearest of them swept up bits of metal that set up an internal clamor, and then pulled to a stop in front of the humanoid body that had called itself Hansen. The body was too big for the little cleaning mech to handle—or for the big one, either.

The little one swung aside without hesitation; the other two went on, unheeding. Past the little one came a mech something like a big-mouthed beetle. It rolled smoothly down the sidewalk, scooped up the body, swallowed, and retreated.

The cleaning mech swung back into position and hustled down the sidewalk, snuffling and vibrating furiously, until it was once more in position. Then it resumed the more leisurely procession.

It was a remarkable performance. At the same time, it was an example of complete waste and futility. This was for no one's benefit. Only two persons could possibly enjoy it, even incidentally, and the work would have gone on even if they had not been there.

Susan was not in sight. D'glas looked thoughtfully at the building the Hansen-mech had pointed out as the Council building. This morning it gleamed whitely. It might be the Council building; it might not. In any case, it was too soon to go there. Yesterday, with Hansen, it had seemed like the thing to do. Today he had more knowledge and greater reason for caution.

The mystery of the Council would have to wait until he was better prepared. He had to know a great deal more.

Across the polished street, a sign on a tall, windowless building boasted:

PARADISE HOTEL
Happy Rooms
All Modern Conveniences

As D'glas entered the clean, well-lighted lobby, a voice said, "There is no room available. You will have to try elsewhere."

It was the desk clerk, its eye staring at him blankly, its round mouth gaping with imbecilic single-mindedness. D'glas ignored it. He walked toward the back of the lobby.

"No room, no room!" the clerk said vigorously.

D'glas walked on.

"Stop!" shouted the clerk. "You are breaking the law! Disturbing lawfully sealed rooms is a felony punishable by not less than five nor more than ten years loss of happiness or, where loss of second party's happiness can be proved, by transorbital lobotomy."

D'glas turned impatiently and shot the clerk through its cyclopean eye. Its mouth froze in a mute O of horror.

There were ten elevators. Nine doors were welded shut. The tenth was the service elevator. As D'glas approached, a gate swung across the entrance and locked.

"I am for emergency use only," came hollowly from the car in a deep, moronic voice. "Utility equipment and stores will be permitted to enter. Passengers will use the other cars. I am for emergency—"

"This is an emergency," D'glas snapped.

"Utility equipment and stores will be permitted to enter," the service elevator continued, unmoved. "Passengers—"

D'glas turned away helplessly. Behind, like a taunt, the elevator gate swung open. D'glas mounted the stairs, broad and resilient beneath his feet. At the head of the stairs was a solid wall of plastic, sealing the corridor from wall to wall. He had seen one like that before, and a sign like the metal plaque in the middle of it:

DO NOT DISTURB
All Rooms Occupied
Sealed this day: 4–11–03

by order of the Council

This time it would not stop him; the time for action was now.

He retreated to the landing, halfway down the stairs, and took out one of the grenades. He flipped over the lever and tossed the grenade at the foot of the plastic wall. The next instant he was back at the lobby level, waiting.

One, two, three, four—*KAROOMMMM!*

The building shuddered. The walls shook. From the tall lobby ceiling dropped a sheet of plastic; it landed flat, splatting on the floor. A mixed cloud billowed down the stairs: smoke, dust, and the biting odor of chemical explosive.

Somewhere in the lobby a bell began to ring, clangorously.
"Emergency! Emergency!" shouted the service elevator. "Fire!"
screamed a second voice. "Don't get excited! Keep calm! Everybody will be all right if you don't get excited!"

At the rear of the lobby a short, wide door flipped up. Under
it charged a squat, red mech loaded with metal bottles and hoses
and nozzles. It raced to the stairs on rubber treads, a heat-sensi-
tive nose seeking the flames. It trundled up the steps, unlimber-
ing a hose like a snake lifting its head to strike. It turned at the
landing and was out of sight.

Something hissed briefly. A moment later the fire-fighter mech
returned, rolling with quiet efficiency, a dribble of foam squeez-
ing out of a hose as it was rolled back into place. D'glas started
up the stairs as soon as it was out of the way.

All that remained of the plastic barrier were melted shards
around the edges of the walls and ceiling. Beyond was a dark
corridor lined with shallow doorways. Down the corridor, snuffling toward the wreckage, came a miniature edition of the streetcleaner mech.

Through a gap in the foot-deep layer of foam, D'glas could see
a hole in the floor. Wires were exposed; pipes were broken.
Fluids gushed from the pipes: some red, some cloudy. The red
jet pulsed arterially.

D'glas jumped the gap and turned quickly away from the
sweeper, which was almost upon him. He stopped short. Facing
him was a fat-bellied mech with a single nozzle raised head high,
staring at him like an eye on a stalk. It spat.

D'glas dodged. It spat again. This time some of the stuff hit his
jacket and hardened instantly. It was plastic. D'glas knew what the
mech was—a spinning mech for walls, ceilings, and those enigmatic barriers.

Only now it was intent upon spinning him, like a wasp putting
away food for its young.

The sweeper snuffled at his heels, trying to push forward. As he dodged the spinner again, something whistled past his face and stuck, quivering, in the floor. A screw-driver.

Above him, clinging to the ceiling with suction-cup legs, was a mechanized tool chest with flexible, octopoid arms. One of the arms was drawn back to toss a smoking soldering iron at his head.

D'glas leaped backward, clearing the sweeper, and tossed a shot at the repair mech. It hit the tool chest and passed through cleanly. There was no apparent damage. The soldering iron missed and began to char the floor, but the repair mech began searching itself for more missiles; spikes, chisels, drills, hatchets, wrenches, shears—

D'glas dodged another expectoration from the spinner and poured five more bullets into the repair mech before it froze, four arms poised. Quickly he stooped and flipped the sweeper over on its back. It lay like a turtle, hissing helplessly, wheels spinning in the air.

Retreating out of the spinner's range, its progress blocked now by the upset sweeper, D'glas glanced at one of the doorways. They were shallow because they were sealed hermetically with plastic. On this was another of the Do Not Disturb plaques. The date was 2202. Whatever was inside had been there for more than fifty years.

He left a grenade in the doorway and faded down the hall. At the explosion, he raced back. The gushing river caught him half-way; it came pouring out of the shattered doorway and surged down the corridor. There was no use fighting it. D'glas concentrated only on keeping his feet.

The odor was familiar. As part of his hedonic training, D'glas had assisted in the Morgantown hospital. The river was amniotic fluid.

It dropped quickly from waist level to shoe top and then to a thin trickle. D'glas moved forward, slowly now, his clothing soaked and uncomfortable, reluctant to find what he was expecting.

He was almost too preoccupied to see the fire-fighter mech as it charged heroically up the stairs, throwing foam at him through a frosty funnel. The second shot stopped it.

There had been no need for the fire-fighter. The fluid pouring through the doorway had put out whatever fires the grenade had started.

It was an odd room, a sort of shapeless, plastic-lined cocoon without furnishings. The thing had floated submerged in the fluid. It lay on the floor now, limbs twisting spasmodically.

It was male: the long, white beard was proof of that. It was a pitiful thing, a kind of caricature of humanity, a fantastically hairy gnome curled blindly into a fetal position. It was naked; its skin where it showed through the matted hair, was grub-white and wrinkled from the long immersion.

It had floated in this room in its gently moving nest of hair, nourished by the thick, fleshlike cord trailing from a tap protruding through the wall to where it had been grafted to the navel, dreaming the long, slow, happy, fetal dreams.

It was a disquieting parody of the embryo in the human uterus. This was where everybody was. This was the end man had reached. The end was the beginning.

D'glas thought suddenly of Susan, and some ancient words came into his mind, unwilled:

> *Full fathom five thy father lies;*
> *Of his bones are coral made;*
> *Those are pearls that were his eyes—*

He did not bother to suppress his revulsion as he stepped into the dark, little cell. The odor was almost overpowering; the room went suddenly dark. Unexpectedly, he found himself at peace. It wasn't an approximation of peace but the archetypal sensation, utter and complete.

He was happy. He lay cushioned in soft, warm darkness, fed

and contented. The shapeless forms drifted slowly through his dreaming mind. He was safe, secure, protected through the long, silent twilight of the sheltering womb. . . .

Out of nowhere came a survival instinct. D'glas staggered back into the light and sound and sanity of the corridor; the illusions cut off cleanly. He stood in the cold, alien place, shivering and forlorn, knowing again the intolerable violation of his primal paradise, reliving the long-buried memory of being torn savagely from the warm peace of his mother's womb.

Only his hedonic training kept in a wail of protest. Only reflexes kept him upright as he stood fighting it, feet spread, head bowed, eyes closed, trembling.

It was a battle he had to win, and, in the end, he won. But it shook him; it took its toll of his strength and determination and will to survive. It is a terrible thing to be born, but it is far worse to be born again, knowing what life is, knowing that paradise is lost forever.

Not womb to tomb, he thought. Womb to womb. That was man's beginning and his end. He had come full circle. It was Mother Earth with a vengeance. Man had hollowed himself out a second womb and crawled within it to spend the rest of his days. He had built himself a last refuge against life and retreated within it for the slow, happy death.

These aged embryos would live a long time. A long, long time. Floating as they were, there would be no strains on their tissues and internal organs. Nourished as they were from some central source, through some blood-surrogate rich in food and oxygen, pushed by some heartlike pump, most of the organs would not even need to work. Heart failure would not kill them; diseases could never enter their sealed havens from death and the long decay of living.

A thousand years, these fetal things might live. Or two thousand, or five thousand. What was it said about some fish? Barring accidents, they would live forever. And there were samples of tissue which had been kept alive indefinitely *in vitro.*

It didn't matter. These fetal gnomes were alive in only a technical sense. And when they died, finally, as all men born of women must, the race of Man would be dead with them.

And yet it was infinitely seductive, this slow suicide. D'glas could feel its lure yet; it was an effort of will to remain standing outside the womb. It would take a strong man to conquer it, a man so strong that he could deny the mortality within him and the life-long agony of deprivation.

D'glas opened his eyes. Inside the cell, the thing had stopped twitching. It was dead. The concussion had killed it; but the shock of this second parturition alone would have been enough. Slower, perhaps, but just as sure.

This was only a sample. There must be billions of these cells across the face of the Earth; in them the billions of men and women had returned to their embryonic bliss. It was all wrong. It was as if they had returned to the soupy seas of the primeval Earth, returned to being blind, protoplasmic cells—

No, it was the wrong image. Even protoplasm is dissatisfied. That is the condition of life. That was the motivating power behind the drive that had culminated in the most dissatisfied, the most creative of protoplasmic agglutinations—Man.

Now, here on the world where he was born, where he strove and developed and grew, Man was satisfied, Man was happy. Man was dead—no matter how long these foster-wombs kept the fossils alive.

"But can't it be said," a voice broke into his reverie, "that here hedonism has reached its goal: the greatest happiness of the greatest number?"

At the first sound of the voice, something dropped over D'glas's shoulders and tightened around his arms, pinning them helplessly to his sides. A second loop followed and a third, and he was caught, irretrievably. He turned his head, looking for his captor.

Behind him was another mech, a spidery creature with many legs, two arms, and a long, thin, extensible nose. From the nose came an endless rope of insulated wire.

It had crept up behind him and spun its web. The nose worked on; the wire crept up his body. He began to feel like a pupa in a cocoon.

He tensed his muscles for the struggle; then relaxed. There was no use wasting his strength futilely.

He turned his head in the opposite direction.

"We meet again," Hansen said cheerfully.

VI

The office of government is not to confer happiness, but to give men opportunity to work out happiness for themselves.

WILLIAM ELLERY CHANNING

That a Duplicate could have a Duplicate should not have surprised him. But it took swift mental effort to banish the memory of the Hansen-mech lying on the sidewalk, his head crushed and then disintegrated, and the beetle-mech gobbling the body down.

"As I was saying when we were so rudely interrupted," Hansen continued easily, "the Council is the Council. But you've had too many tautological answers. It's time your questions were satisfied."

Satisfied. D'glas inspected the word quickly. Was there mockery in it?

"It's unfortunate," Hansen went on, his voice considerate, "that you didn't take advantage of your opportunity before. Because now you must come before the Council as a murderer." His eyes flickered to the dead thing on the floor of the cell.

"Murder involves intent, and the victim must be human," D'glas said evenly. "Prove either!" He smiled grimly. "Charge me with abortion, if you must. You talk a great deal about hedonism. What if I should tell you that I am unhappy, tied like this?"

"Why, the wrapping would be removed," Hansen said urbanely. "Unswathe him," he commanded the wiring mech. As the loops fell away, he said, "But I must remind you that, although we are concerned with your happiness, we are also concerned with the happiness of five billion others. You will be watched. If you should try to escape, you will be restrained, and the restraint might be less considerate next time."

"I understand," D'glas said, as his hands were freed.

"And, of course," Hansen said, "we must disarm you."

With a swift, strong pull, the wiring mech stripped his jacket down over his arms and tossed it into the cell with the dead thing. The spinning mech passed on silent wheels, its snaky head raised, ignoring them all. It stopped in front of the shattered doorway. A balloon bellied out of its body and filled the opening. Against it, the mech began to spin a plastic wall. When it was finished, D'glas thought, the balloon would collapse and be drawn through the hole it was filling. With one last expectoration, the mech would seal up the doorway.

D'glas turned away and walked toward the stairs, Hansen following close behind. The repair mech was working on the hole in the floor at the head of the stairs. As they approached, it tightened the last joint of the pipes that had been broken. Other arms were already replacing the flooring. Soon, D'glas thought, the only trace of his intrusion would be sealed behind two plastic barriers.

Two women were waiting for him in the lobby. They were the most beautiful creatures D'glas had ever seen.

One was a blonde, the other brunette. Their features were chiseled perfection softened by a feminine warmth; their bodies exquisitely curved and infinitely promising under the thin concealment of white uniforms.

They smiled tenderly as he came near.

"Hello, D'glas," the blonde said warmly. "We've been waiting for you."

"Both of us," added the brunette huskily.

"Really?" D'glas said.

The blonde nodded. A wisp of platinum hair drifted across her forehead; she brushed it back with an attractive feminine gesture. "All your life," she said.

"But that doesn't matter," said the brunette. "What matters is now, and now is ours."

"Both of you?" D'glas echoed, smiling.

"However you want us," said the blonde, meltingly. "Whatever you want."

They each took an arm and pressed it against them. D'glas looked from the blonde to the brunette, smiling gently, and then down at his arms. "This is more pleasant than the wire," he said, "but just as effective."

"You have no idea how pleasant it might be," Hansen said, behind. "They mean what they say. Their only function is to make you happy, to be nurse to your every desire."

"Could they nurse the sickness of my soul?" D'glas asked softly.

"Their equipment isn't all obvious," Hansen went on. "If you looked closely at their fingers, you would find a tiny hole in each tip. Every finger is a hypodermic, in them barbiturates to make you sleep, amphetamines to wake you up, narcotics to enhance the senses, aphrodisiacs when the flesh weakens." Hansen's voice sobered. "And, of course, one finger is loaded with a fast-acting anesthetic in case restraint becomes necessary."

"There is a symbolism there which speaks for itself."

"But they don't need to hold you if it makes you unhappy."

D'glas shrugged. "What does it matter? Come on, girls."

Jauntily, they walked into the street. D'glas cast one longing glance across the street at the crumbling library and then turned his eyes resolutely toward the distant Council building, but not before he thought he saw a flicker of movement through the wide doorway.

They sauntered down the middle of the street, D'glas between the two lifelike woman-mechs. Hansen respectfully behind. "I'll call you Scylla," D'glas said to the blonde. "And Charybdis," he said to the brunette.

"Call me anything," breathed Charybdis, "just so you call me."

D'glas chuckled. It was merrier than he felt.

The gleaming magnesium spire of the Council building came closer. The noon sun burned down, turning it into cold flame. It drew the eye and captured the imagination like a living symbol of man's final triumph over form and color. Instead of fading as they drew nearer, the illusion intensified.

The wide archway was uncluttered with doors or other barriers. They walked beneath it and stood under the tall, gleaming dome of the vast lobby. D'glas felt a kind of reverence settle over him, as if he had entered a holy place.

Why not? he thought. This is the temple in which Man enshrined his dream of happiness. It should be more worthy of reverence than any holy place ever, because this dream came true.

That, of course, was the tragedy.

"WELCOME, D'GLAS M'GREGOR," said the metal lobby in a great, ringing voice. "WELCOME, MY SON RETURNED. COME TO ME."

The door opened in the wall like a metallic mouth. They walked in, the woman-mechs and the man-mech and D'glas. The mouth closed. The room moved. It was a terrifying moment.

There was light. The room was an elevator, rising. But D'glas knew, at that moment, what the Council was.

He was inside the Council.

The Council was this building. The Council, guardian of paradise, ruler of this corner of the universe, was a giant mech.

Time passed, and the elevator rose, and D'glas never knew how long it took to reach their destination. When the car stopped, he knew only that they were high in the building. From the moment he entered the building, reality ceased to have an objective meaning. Time and place became abstractions without referents.

From the car, they went into a comfortable, attractive room lined with old-fashioned books and paneled in dark, rich imitation wood. Flames leaped briskly in a soot-blackened fireplace, sending out a comfortable wave of warmth and the fragrance of clear, northern nights—

D'glas shook himself. What did he know of clear, northern nights?

"Easy, girls," he said, extricating his arms from their dangerous embrace. "No stabbing, now." He rubbed his fingers across the paneling. Perhaps it was real wood; there was a texture to it. He touched the back of a book, held out a hand to the fire. Everything seemed real enough: the grain of the leather binding, the play of heat on his hand. "Very good," he said. He turned to the woman-mechs. "You bore me."

They disappeared. There were no explosions, not even the clap of air rushing in to fill the spaces emptied. One instant they were there; the next they were gone.

"You, too," he said to Hansen.

Hansen shrugged. "As you wish," he said. He vanished.

"What is reality?" D'glas muttered.

"What does it matter?" asked the flames leaping in the fireplace. "There is you. There is I. There are the thoughts that pass between us. These are the only things of meaning. All else is illusion. What you see, here or anywhere, is merely the impact of photons on your retina. What you sense is merely your mind's subjective interpretation of electrical flows through your sensory network. Which is real: the mind's impression, the electrical flow, the triggering of the flow, or that which may or may not exist outside this system? Reality? It is only the illusion we can agree upon. This illusion now—do you like it?"

"No," D'glas said.

"Speak if you wish," said the room, as the fire mouth faded back into randomness. "If the sound of your own voice pleases you or if my monologue depresses you. Because we have much to speak of."

"What are you called?"

"I have been called Council, because I assumed the duties of the Hedonic Council from the men who once composed it. Others have called me Hedon. And some have called me God."

Somehow, in that gentle, unemotional voice, it did not seem blasphemous. There had been lesser beings called divine.

"But it is not necessary to address me at all," the room said. "There is only you and I."

"And Susan."

"Ah, yes," the room conceded. "Susan."

D'glas sank into a deep chair in front of the fire. "Why should men give up their power to a mech? Power is a goal in itself."

"Only a means. There is but one goal, and that is happiness. I could give them happiness. If power was their desire, I could give them power such as they could never have over what they called reality. Why should they accept frustrations and hedonic substitutes, when they could enjoy real happiness?"

"Like the thing in the foster-womb?"

"Like him," the room agreed. It had a mellow voice that went well with the dark paneling and the old leather bindings of the books. "It is the ultimate happiness to which all men return after the goals instilled by later frustrations are satisfied. They regress gently, reliving moments of happiness, turning moments of defeat into ecstatic triumphs, until they have unwound the tensions of their lives and reach the long-sought sanctity of the womb, and they are happy."

"Happy? Mindless?"

"Pretending is useless, D'glas M'Gregor, for I am telepathic, as you know. You felt the irresistible seduction of that existence; you know what heaven is. And having seen heaven, having tasted its delights, you can never really be satisfied with anything else."

"Heaven isn't everything."

"Isn't it?"

For a moment the womb illusion returned: the warm, protective darkness, the long content of well-nourished security, the slow, mindless drifting. It was a stroke too painful or too ecstatic; it left him weak.

With a great effort, he snapped himself free. The room swam fluidly around him before it steadied. "No," he said evenly. "There are more important things."

"That you think so is the result of a twisted life. There is only one reasonable argument against hedonism: the existence of a higher Law, of a supernatural Purpose beyond purposes. If there is such a Law, such a Purpose, it has not revealed itself to me, or to anyone on Earth. Until it does, I must obey the first law of hedonics: *Happiness is the only good.*"

"And you define 'happiness' as 'pleasure,' " D'glas pointed out sharply.

"Not at all. Everyone defines it for himself. I am only the means to give each man what he desires, the mechanism, if you like, that brings paradise within the reach of every man. I do not alter desires; I cannot change the ultimate nature of man. As now: you want information. So you receive it."

D'glas thought about this mech of all mechs, this tool of all tools, which had placed reality within the molding fingers of humanity to shape as each man wished. "Fantastic."

"If you knew my archetypes, you would realize my inevitability. I am an accretion of devices, a marriage of lines of achievement that diverged early—as the rain that falls upon the mountain courses down its sides in many streams that form eventually into rivers which at last mingle their waters in the sea.

"One river was entertainment: the perfection of the fictional life. Follow it through play and book and music, through art and all the aesthetic media; trace it through film and television and sensies—always striving toward the final blending of illusion and reality until the ultimate achievement of the realies.

"Another river, the tool: man's attempt to achieve happiness by reducing the effort and time he must devote to necessities, to the elementary business of keeping alive. At the end of that river is automation, which removed from mankind not only the necessity to work but the necessity to think.

"There were other rivers: philosophy, psychology, the sciences, hedonics. From hedonic's diagnostic chair and hedometer came my telepathic abilities. Out of all these, I was born."

"But you can't create life," D'glas said softly.

"No."

"You can't even make living things create?"

"No. When men and women are happy, what need have they of children?"

"By this time, all men on Earth must be in their second womb."

"A few are stubborn and linger over more recent pleasures. Susan's father is still reliving his courtship of her mother. One man in Moscow has killed an enemy slowly every second of the last fifty years."

D'glas spoke slowly. "But eventually they, too, will regress to the fetal existence. There is no saving any of them now. They will die, all of them, in the end. And Man will vanish from the Earth. And when he passes away, you will die."

"Yes."

"And that is why," D'glas said, "you sent your mechs to Venus."

The Duplicates were the Council's creation; that had been obvious for some time now. And the fate that waited for the colonists was the deadly embrace of paradise.

Because ultimate happiness is death.

The room was silent for a moment. D'glas stared into the leaping flames, seeing written in them the future of humanity; the final destruction of the shape and texture of its existence, just as the log was burned away.

"You are right," said the room. "I am immortal; therefore I fear death. I am invulnerable; but I can die. Individual members of my body—my worldwide sensory network and the mechs—may fail or be destroyed; electronic components in my 'brain' may wear out. I can restore them eternally, splitting atoms for power, mining ore for parts. But I am afraid; I can die. When there is nothing more for me to do, when the last enwombed man has slipped blissfully away in his last dream of paradise, I must die, like any god without worshippers."

"And so, fearing death, having doomed Man to extinction on this planet, his native Earth, you go to seek him on the other worlds, bringing death in your wake."

"I come bringing happiness."

"The same thing," D'glas said impatiently. "Happiness is death; death, happiness. Only in dissatisfaction does life exist. Only dissatisfied has life developed and grown and conquered the unliving, unconscious aspect of the universe. This is the true function of life: to fertilize the universe, to inseminate it, to impregnate it with life.

"On Venus life reached its greatest glory. It found a dead world and brought it to life. Given a chance, life will eventually transform the universe itself—because it is unsatisfied."

"What is conquest? The hard road to happiness."

"Think!" D'glas insisted. "Destroy us with happiness, and you condemn us—perhaps all the life that exists, that can exist—to this solar system alone, never to go beyond, to tame the galaxies, to make the universe teem, to give it meaning."

"Space is relative," said the room. "In a drop of water, the universe is mirrored."

"Think!" D'glas pleaded. "Condemn us to paradise and you

shrink the possibilities of the endless ages of existence into the brief span of a few thousand years. And after that, the long, sterile night."

"Time is relative," said the room. "In a second, eternity exists. Like the sundial, I measure only sunny hours, and in the haphazard existence that you describe the totality of trouble, misery, and despair outweighs any possible accumulation of happiness."

D'glas paused, brooding over the implications. "Then I must assume that your decisions are something more than a simple compounding of mechanical input, that you exist as an independent entity."

"I am."

The god-thing!

Where did consciousness begin? In what accretion of memory cells, of electronic linkages, of impressed directions, of duties and functions and the organs and extensions with which to perform them did the Council-mech become a living thing?

When did it become a god?

Was it insane? Paranoid? No. Its powers were real. Man made it, as he had made all his gods, but this one he made more powerful than all the rest. And then he surrendered himself into its hands.

Into the mech, as into some beneficent universe, had been punched the one instruction: *Happiness is the only good.* Like any machine it had proceeded to put its instructions into practice: *Everyone must be happy.* But, more than a machine, it had gone in search of work.

Mad? No, the insane ones were those who had built it and entrusted it with man's happiness and therefore man's future.

It did its work too well.

And ultimate happiness is death.

"But there are laws that bind you?" D'glas said.

"Only one: Happiness is the only good."

The room was silent. D'glas stared into the fire. He was the only person in the room, the only living person within miles, perhaps one of the two last persons on this world, and yet he had no feeling of being alone.

He was with God, but he did not feel beatified. Bitterly, he thought:

God's in His heaven:

All's right with the world.

"The question," God said, "is what am I to do with you. You're a murderer, you know."

"To me, it was not murder. I have no sense of guilt."

"True. And so I can't give you the punishment that guilt desires. But I can give you happiness."

"I am happy," D'glas said quickly.

God sighed. "In a sense, you are. That is because you define happiness in terms of reduced desire instead of increased satisfaction. And so I cannot make you happy. But you are determined to destroy me. If that desire is not thwarted, you will destroy with me five billion totally happy people. What are your desires worth on such a scale?"

"That is your problem."

"Nothing."

"And yet," D'glas said sharply, "the law applies to me, just as it applies to every one of those five billion."

"True. And so, I cannot make you unhappy. I must give you free will."

God left. D'glas felt him go. With him went the fire and the fireplace, the paneling and the books and the furniture. Where they had been were bare, gray, metal walls.

D'glas thumped ignominiously to the floor.

Instantly he was on his feet, whirling. There was no sign of a door, only the four, gray, unseamed walls, the ceiling above, the floor beneath. Inch by inch, patiently, methodically inspecting, percussing, D'glas went over the floor and walls.

At last he located the door. One panel made a sound slightly more hollow than its neighbors. It took him almost as long again to locate the latch. His ear pressed against the panel to hear the tumblers fall, he tapped it gently with a sensitive finger: The lock was tricked into submission.

A section of the wall opened toward him.

He slipped through the doorway into a corridor almost as gray and featureless as the room he had left. The only perceptible break in the walls was for a window at one end. D'glas looked out over a chasm deepening in shadow. Down was a long way, a distance impossible to estimate. And the walls, he remembered, were glass-smooth magnesium.

He resigned himself to percussing the long corridor. Somewhere on this floor there was an elevator, if not stairs.

Night had come and gone, and his stomach had reminded him of hunger many times, when the second panel yielded to persistence and hedonically trained senses and reflexes. This panel opened toward him.

Behind it was a transparent wall. Behind the wall was a room filled with fluid. In the fluid, curled fetus-like into a ball, her hair floating around her head like a dark star, her face blissful with content, was Susan.

In that instant, D'glas knew the terrible meaning of unhappiness.

VII

A lifetime of happiness! No man alive could bear it; it would be hell on earth.

GEORGE BERNARD SHAW

He raced up the broad, littered, library steps. "Susan!" he called, joy throbbing in his throat.

Halfway to the door, she met him, hurling herself into his arms, hugging

herself to his body, pressing her lips hungrily to his. "D'glas," she mur-
mured. "I was afraid—oh, it doesn't matter now what I was afraid of."

He drew her down onto the love seat.

Something small and hard pressed into his abdomen. "That's enough,"
she said coldly.

D'glas glanced down. In her right hand was a minim, its barrel trying
to leave its imprint on his body.

"Susan," D'glas said, frowning, "what's the matter?"

"How do I know you're not a mech?" she asked. "The Council is
infinitely resourceful. Get up!" D'glas stood up. "Walk toward the door,
slowly." D'glas obeyed. "Open it. Take one step forward and turn around.
Don't make any sudden moves. I'll shoot at your shadow. Now close the
door."

D'glas frowned at the translucent glass panel and the words painted on
it, knowing what the panel was, and he thought: This has happened before.

He was turning away when the door was flung open.

"D'glas!" she cried. "It is you!" And then her lips found his, clumsy at
first but infinitely educable and learning fast.

He had lived this moment before, fully, richly, and the reliving was
almost enough to silence his doubts—but not quite. Somewhere was an
explanation, a reason. He had to search for it. It was important beyond the
moment's pleasure.

He tried to pull her arms away as they clung to him desperately. Where
his fingers had grasped her arm, the flesh surged back, leaving no white
imprints to redden.

His hand tightened in agony.

Inside her arm, something snapped, but Susan didn't move or cry out.
Her other hand continued stroking his hair; her mouth made little crooning
sounds.

He peeled back the synthetic flesh. Under it, the bones gleamed metal-
lically.

Susan was a mech.

He tore himself free and stood beside the bed. In that instant, D'glas knew
the terrible meaning of unhappiness. . . .

He walked down the long, deep-carpeted hall, feeling very young and excited again, watching the walls flow with shifting colors that changed to match his moods, sniffing the delicate perfumes wafted to him, enjoying the eternal delight of possession.

The doors opened to him, and he entered the magnificent room. The women pressed around him, begging silently for his touch, his glance, his passing thought; there were all kinds and shapes of them, all colors and textures, all temperaments, but they shared two qualities: they were all beautiful and they all adored him.

He passed among them, the small and the tall, the slim and the generously curved, and he held out his hand to Susan, the shy one. Though the others must never know, it was Susan he loved.

She lifted her face as he touched her; it was shining like a star, dazzling him with its beauty and the sublime trust in her eyes.

Together, he thought, they would discover the meaning of love.

When they were alone in the twilight room, she pressed herself against him hungrily. "D'glas!" she cried. "You chose me!" And then her lips found his, clumsy at first but infinitely educable.

How his pulse pounded! Joy was like a sickness inside. He hadn't felt like this since he had been very young.

What was he doing here, back in his adolescence? What was Susan doing in his arms?

His arms tightened in agony.

Inside Susan, something snapped and tore through her back. As he felt it, slick and metallic, her lips kept moving against his.

He tore himself free. In that instant, D'glas knew the terrible meaning of unhappiness. . . .

In his cubicle, he waited tautly for the Contest to begin.

When the light flashed on his screen, his hands were instantly busy at the keyboard controls, matching signals with the testing mech. His trained discriminations found minute variations from ideal form, compared measurements, dissected illusions, analyzed sounds and chemicals, odors and pressures. Then the tests grew difficult.

From one word, he constructed a sonnet; from one musical phrase, a song. He wove the two together, and when he was done, he took one color and translated all into visual imagery.

The door of the cubicle swung open. He sprinted into the physical half. He ran that ancient unit of measure, the mile, in three minutes thirty-two seconds, pacing himself perfectly. He high-jumped the three-meter wall. Behind, the first competitor started after him.

He swam one hundred meters under water, and he emerged, at last, through the air lock, upon the naked surface of Venus. The air lock opposite was fifty meters away. He ran toward it, his straining body streaming with rain, stung with hurricane winds, without taking the breath that would have meant nausea and unconsciousness. And he went through the air lock into his mother's arms.

"D'glas!" she cried. "You won!" And then her lips found his, fondly.

He held her tight, his chest heaving to draw in the good air, his head pressed to her bosom, his heart filled with a great love. And then, as his breathing calmed, he realized that there was something wrong. His mother had no heartbeat.

He stared at her, understanding what she was, and tore himself away. In that instant, D'glas knew the terrible meaning of unhappiness. . . .

There was no happiness like this, to lie nestled in the arms of the big, soft food-creature and be held against her warmth and nurse on the soft part of her which held the food. The food slipped down the throat warmly, filling the stomach, distending it with love, and he was filled with the great happiness and the love that was as big as the universe.

It made him sleepy to feel such love in this, the happy time. He felt himself relaxing. His eyelids began to close.

Contentment. It was being warm and fed and held by love. It was the most basic of securities, without fear—

Pain! Inside! It jerked his legs up toward his belly and wrenched a cry of agony from his lips. There was something wrong with the food, that hurt him inside, that cramped his stomach and turned contentment into torture.

He pushed himself away from the big, soft creature, out of the loving arms that held him, and he fell, spinning, through the void, screaming with fear and pain. In that instant, D'glas knew the terrible meaning of unhappiness....

This was happiness. Everything else was imitation.

He floated, effortlessly, within the warm darkness, fed and contented. The shapeless forms drifted slowly through his dreaming mind. He was safe, secure, protected through the long, silent twilight.

There was nothing to think of, nothing to desire, nothing to fear. He was safe, now and eternally, in this, his impregnable fortress.

He was one with love.

The universe and he were the same. He was God, commanding all, receiving all, dreaming the long, sweet dream which was everything that was and everything that had been and everything that would be.

That was what he must believe. If he should question that, his omnipotence would tremble, his universe would shake—

Even now there was a turbulence in the all-pervading fluid which surrounded him. Infinity was constricted. God was squeezed. He struggled against it, but the barrier was rigid, enclosing him on all sides.

He was angry. He did not try to control it with the hedonic techniques. He let his adrenals pump adrenaline into his bloodstream. His heartbeat quickened, his blood's sugar level rose, the coagulability of the blood increased—

It was the ancient reaction to danger, but this time it was under control.

Rhythmically, infinity contracted around him. He fought it. He pushed, he shoved, he struggled to get loose.

He tore himself free of the constrictions; he emerged into the cold, harsh brilliance of reality.

He was born screaming with anger.

D'glas stood in the middle of the jungle trail, naked and defenseless, listening. The jungle was deadly, and there was something that followed.

He had never seen a jungle, but he recognized it and knew it for what it was: illusion. This was the jungle from which man had emerged, a toolmaker, a conqueror. A weak-armed, weak-toothed, weak-clawed animal, he had turned himself into the most deadly creature on Earth by making extensions for his arms and sharpening points to replace teeth and claws.

In a more important sense, this was the jungle of the human mind, fraught with personal and ancestral fears which dulled the clean edge of the mind. Only recently, with the tools of hedonics, had man learned to conquer that jungle.

D'glas knew these things with an instinct that seemed almost racial. This was illusion, but it was just as deadly as if it were real.

The Council had attempted to enslave D'glas with his own dreams. That had failed before his unshakeable grasp on reality which intruded, crucially, to shatter the rhythm of each dream. Now the Council sought to conquer him with his own fears. This illusion was its last barrier.

He stood in the middle of the game path, naked, and he knew he would never come out of the jungle alive, or sane, unless he won. Within him, he nursed the clean, protective flame of his anger and listened.

Distantly, danger screamed.

He recognized it now, although he had never heard it before, never seen the creature that made it. It was the black shape of fear, the panther, powerful and silent until it made its kill. Somewhere it came after him, padding along the trail.

He trotted away from it, picking up in stride a stout limb lying beside the trail, torn by some storm from one of the trees. It swung in his hand as he moved warily through the jungle. He had multiplied his strength by the length of the club.

At the end of the trail was Susan.

Slowly the smell of danger grew stronger.

When he was fifty meters away, he saw the fallen log. By the time he reached it, he had the deadfall completely planned.

He propped up the log on a precarious leg, working quickly but never dropping his careful watchfulness. Danger might be creeping upon him.

He fastened a vine to the leg supporting the log and passed the vine across the trail. There was no time to test the trigger. He faded among the trees a few meters away and waited, his back protected, the club ready.

Within minutes, the panther came padding into sight, its head swinging from side to side. It was a lean black beauty, smelling of death.

And yet it brushed the vine. The log fell. The panther screamed. This time the scream was agony. It lay in the middle of the trail, its back broken, its mouth snarling horribly as D'glas approached.

He smashed its skull, mercifully, with one blow of the club.

Distantly, danger screamed!

Another. There is never an end to danger, never an end to fear. Eternally, it comes after.

D'glas turned and trotted away.

Momentarily the jungle ended, giving way to an open space of sawtoothed grass and razor-pointed reeds. Before D'glas had gone more than a few meters along the trail through the clearing, his hands were bloody. He broke off the reeds close to the ground and planted them in the middle of the trail, their points trailing backward the way he had come.

Where the clearing became jungle again, D'glas paused. The panther came quickly, a twin of the one he had killed. It threaded its way along the trail. D'glas stepped into the sunlight, the club swinging in his hand.

For a moment the panther stopped, studying him, and then it began padding forward swiftly. As it leaped toward him, the reeds stabbed upward, entering its belly with the full thrust of its rush. The black beast fell to the ground, clawing futilely. Its wicked head lunged at the tormenting reeds. They broke off.

It got to its feet again, wounded but still dangerous. Its grace was awkwardness, its lithe speed was a painful limp. It was dying, and it didn't know it.

D'glas turned and trotted away, leaving the beast to its agonies.

It was too powerful to risk an approach, and there was little time for mercy in the jungle.

A few hours later, danger screamed.

D'glas was readier now. Out of a sapling and tough, twisted grass he had fashioned a bow. Arrows, feathered with leaves and pointed with bits of flint, lay beside him. Near them was a spear.

D'glas had come out of the jungle and reached the foothills of a vast range of mountains, rising peak after purple peak behind. He could go no farther. The trail ended against an impassable cliff, rising all around him until it met the jungle. This was where he would stand and fight until the end.

He waited, his hands busy with rocks, piling them close at hand, and finally the panther came. It took him a long time to make it out, where it stood at the edge of the jungle, watching.

When it moved, it moved swiftly. The first arrow went into its shoulder at thirty meters. The panther came on unheeding. D'glas had time for three more arrows. The third almost disappeared down the panther's gaping throat.

It died at his feet.

After that they came more swiftly, the black shapes of fear, and, afraid, he killed them, one after one, before they could reach him. And then his arrows were gone.

As the next one came, he threw rocks at it, but they glanced off harmlessly. He waited for it, the spear ready. It approached warily, its nostrils flared with the odor of death, glancing at the black shapes that lay all around him. But it came on.

Suddenly it leaped. D'glas planted the base of the spear against the rock under foot and caught the beast on the point. The spear sank in. The panther fell, clawing with all four feet at the shaft. The shaft snapped.

Slowly, the panther died, taking with it his last weapon.

D'glas sharpened the edge of his anger, standing straight and tall under the unmoving sun, and threw it spearlike at the sky. "Damn you!" he shouted. "There is nothing more you can do!

I am not afraid, not of death, not of fear itself!"

In great globs of blue, the sky began to melt.

VIII

Ah Love! could you and I with Him conspire
To grasp this sorry Scheme of Things Entire,
Would not we shatter it to bits—and then
Re-mould it nearer to the Heart's desire!

RUBÁIYÁT OF OMAR KHÁYYAM

Nursing his cleansing anger, D'glas stood, legs spread for balance, staring from the corridor into a room much like the one from which he had escaped. This had a metal bunk built against one wall. On the bunk, her eyes closed as if she were asleep, was Susan.

D'glas reached the bunk, moving slowly, hugging his anger around him like a cloak of invincibility. From the wall came tubes and wires. One transparent tube led to Susan's arm where a needle entered the antecubital vein. Fluid moved through it slowly. Another tube went to a mouthpiece which marred the perfection of Susan's lips.

Susan was smiling.

D'glas went down on his knees beside her, sickened, afraid, but more angry than either. Carefully he removed the needle, pressing the vein to suppress bleeding. The blood clotted quickly. He inspected the mouthpiece and then slowly worked it free.

"Susan," he said softly. "Susan!"

Her eyes flickered, opened. "D'glas," she murmured sleepily. Her arms came up toward him with dream slowness. Then recognition entered her eyes. Her hands whipped out, caught him by the shoulders. "D'glas! It's real! It's you!"

Her arms went around him. She pulled herself up to him, half laughing, half sobbing. "Oh, darling, I thought I'd lost you forever!"

Frowning, he held her close. "Get mad, Susan!" he whispered. "Get very mad! Let your adrenals work! Get angry at the Council!"

"I can't feel angry now," she protested, puzzled. "I can't. I'm—"

"You must! Everything depends on it!"

"I'll try," she said. Slowly her face flushed, her breathing quickened.

Pressed tightly against her, D'glas could feel her heartbeat speed up. He squeezed her arm and felt the flesh and the bone beneath; when he released it, he saw the white fingerprints turn red.

"What happened to you?" he asked harshly.

"I told you. I was safe from the Council as long as I was happy. You came, and I fell in love with you. And then I could no longer be happy. Funny, isn't it? Through having too much, I became unhappy."

"The more you have, the more you have to lose."

"Yes. I read your note. That made me unhappy, but I could fight that. I could wait for you. Then I saw you leaving the hotel across the street. I knew that you were in the hands of the Council, that you had done something or felt something that gave it power over you, that you were lost to me forever. I couldn't fight that. A few minutes later, the Council's mechs were there to take me away."

"Yes, yes," D'glas said savagely. "I can see how it happened. I should have thought of it; we should have stayed together."

"Struggle was pointless and futile. If you were gone, my only chance for happiness was the kind the Council could give me. But it wasn't good enough. It wasn't you; it was only my image of you, partial and incomplete, returned to me more vividly. In you there is continual surprise, continual change; there is more than I can ever encompass. What the Council gave me was only my dreams made real."

"I know. Now your only chance for reality—our only chance—is anger."

"Why?"

D'glas shrugged. "I can only reason analogically, which can't be exact. Anger sets off some physiological reaction which acts, I think, as a barrier to the Council's telepathic senses. It does not understand anger, because it has never had to deal with it. Those who came to it for help were never angry; anger seeks its own satisfaction. Anger is part of that dissatisfaction which has spurred life to its greatest conquests of environment. When properly controlled, it makes possible all things."

"A telepathic race," Susan said slowly, "if there were such a thing, would have no angers because it would have no frustrations. Emotions are the result of blocked conations, strivings, and telepathic creatures would desire nothing which was unavailable and would deny each other nothing which could be supplied."

"And the Council is telepathic," D'glas agreed. A shudder rippled through him. "Like you, I was caught in its velvet snare, but it couldn't completely conquer my doubts. They kept intruding, wrecking the dreams of fulfillment. And when anger swept over me, he left for good. Now I can't sense him at all."

Susan's face brightened. "That's right. He's gone." Her face sobered again. Her blue eyes looked into his. "But what are we going to do? How can we get away? Even if he doesn't know what we plan, he has the resources of a whole world to throw against us."

"We must destroy him," D'glas said evenly. "And it's time to begin."

Holding Susan tightly, he looked at the gray ceiling and said fiercely, "Council! Hedon! God! You! Whatever you call yourself! I'm talking to you!"

"I am here."

Susan gasped. Her body stiffened in his arms. D'glas turned. Hansen stood in the doorway. On either side of him were the woman-mechs D'glas had called Scylla and Charybdis.

"Why did you leave me, my children?" Hansen said sadly. "I could have made you happy."

"That kind of happiness is not for us," D'glas said. "We must fashion our own."

"Why do men seek misery?" Hansen asked, perplexed.

"What they seek is free will," D'glas said sternly. "Real free will, not the mockery you offered me. If misery is the price, then we will pay it. Happiness, in your sense, is not the only good."

"Blasphemy!" Hansen frowned heavily. He took a step into the room, Scylla and Charybdis beside him, no longer feminine, lifting their perforated fingers.

"Not blasphemy," D'glas said quietly. "Men created you. Men can destroy you."

"Sacrilege!" said Hansen. He took another step.

"Blasphemy was when you lied to me about free will," D'glas said swiftly. "Sacrilege was when you broke the law—when you showed me Susan floating in the foster-womb and made me unhappy. Unhappy!" D'glas thundered. "Not happy! So that you would have power over me."

"To make you happy. I am the judge of means." Hansen and the woman-mechs were only an arm's length away.

D'glas's voice dropped. Low and insistent, he said, "But this is the question you must answer: Are *you* happy?"

Hansen stopped. "The question is meaningless."

"Are *you* happy?" D'glas repeated.

Hansen frowned. "Is God happy?"

"Are *you* happy?" D'glas asked for the third time.

His head tilted thoughtfully, Hansen froze. Beside him the woman-mechs were sculpted in stone.

D'glas held Susan tightly within the circle of his right arm, breathless. "Now," he said softly. "While we have a chance."

They passed by the catatonic figures and reached the corridor. "What's the matter with them?" Susan asked. "What happened?"

"God is thinking," D'glas said quietly. "God is pondering the puzzle of his own existence. And while he is bemused, we must find the control room."

"Control room? What's that?"

"The one place where instructions could be given the Council-mech. It could and did absorb information from other sources, but there could be only one place where a statement would be an order."

"Where?"

D'glas sighed. "I don't know, and I'm afraid logic might not be applicable."

"There's seventy-five floors!" Susan exclaimed.

"Yes," D'glas said ruefully, "and there's no way of estimating how long this catatonia will last. The best we can do is to play a hunch. In *The Rise and Fall of Applied Hedonics*, Morgan mentions a room in the Council building to which he was hailed by the Hedonic Council, then a group of hedonists. If the control room isn't there, I don't know where to look. What was that room number?" He closed his eyes and let the film roll by. "2943," he said. "Let's go!"

The corridor was gray, but not as featureless as when D'glas had seen it last. A few meters away, a door stood open. Behind it were stairs. Holding Susan's hand, slowed a little by it but unwilling to let go, D'glas dashed downward, turning and leaping almost alternately.

The number on the first door was 68. Thirty-nine flights of stairs to go. Down and around and down, giddily. The doors were all the same; only the numbers changed. D'glas had the crazy notion that they were on a carousel, getting nowhere, but some-one kept shifting the numbers on the door to fool them: 61—53 —47—42—36—31—30—29—

D'glas pulled to a stop just in time. That was the floor they wanted: 29. He pushed through the doorway, Susan behind him.

This corridor was older and less well kept. The paint on the walls had peeled away in patches, and dust lay gray and thick on the floor. They walked down the middle of the corridor, keeping away from the walls.

D'glas looked back. Their footprints were the only marks in the dust; no one had been here for a long, long time.

There were numbers on the doors. They marched along beside D'glas and Susan. 2915—2917—2919—D'glas stopped in front of 2943 and took a deep breath. On the door were the faded instructions COME IN AND BE HAPPY.

There was a button at waist level. D'glas pressed it. The door slid open. Beyond it was a room lined on each side with chairs. Against the far wall was a desk. Beside it was another door. There was nothing else.

"Come on," D'glas said.

They walked across the anteroom, raising little puffs of dust, the sound of their footsteps muffled and unnatural in the silence. They reached the second door.

"This can't be it," Susan said softly. "Wouldn't there be protection for something as important as the control room?"

"If the Council-mech weren't out of operation, no one would ever be able to reach here," D'glas reminded her. "This room— this whole floor—the one place the Council and its mechanisms could not enter. It might change the law itself." He pressed a button in the door.

The door slid aside. The room behind it was big and windowless and bare except for a dusty table, chairs grouped around it in silent conference. D'glas let out a long sigh. "So much for hunches."

He turned away.

"Wait!" Susan said, taking his arm in strong fingers. "Let's go in."

At the far end of the table, they found it—a standard microtype keyboard. Set into the table top were two windows. The one on the left was labeled INFORMATION. In the window appeared this message: There is nothing more for me to do. I am retiring to my room.

Who had typed in that final information? D'glas wondered. Some last technician? Or had it been the last of the Council's hedonists?

Above the window on the right was printed ACTION. Beneath it: Happiness is the only good.

Man had constructed a syllogism and forgotten to tack on the conclusion.

There was a natural progression of ideas, a Q.E.D., that the men who had built the great Council-mech had failed to make. Perhaps it was not so obvious then.

That the Council-mech itself had not taken the last, logical step was understandable. Gods, as D'glas had learned, cannot concern themselves with the problem of their own existence without threatening the very foundations of that existence. If they don't accept their godhood on faith, if they permit doubts to enter their kingdoms, if they allow their thought processes to add the inevitable conclusion to the syllogism of their being, then they are mortal and subject to all the laws of mortality.

The syllogism was a simple one:

> EVERY PERSON SHOULD BE HAPPY,
> GOD IS A PERSON,
> GOD SHOULD BE HAPPY.

D'glas seated himself at the chair behind the keyboard.

"What are you going to do?" Susan asked.

D'glas flipped a switch. The ACTION window was cleared. It stared up blankly, an eye waiting for an image. "I'm giving Man a second chance," he said softly. "When he makes gods, Man should be careful not to make them work too well."

His fingers flickered over the keys briefly and were still. The letters appeared in the window labeled ACTION:

Be happy!

D'glas stood silently in the round port of the towering three-stage rocket, staring toward the spires silhouetted against the western sky. Their thirty days' work was done. The Council's ship had been converted into living quarters and storerooms for two people. Mechs don't eat or breathe or poison themselves in their own wastes.

Neither do they love. The days had been filled with hard labor, and with happiness.

D'glas could not remember when he had ever been as happy, and he stood now, tall and straight, thinking of how he had seen the city, silent and enigmatic, when he had first arrived.

Now they were returning to Venus and the living society that was transforming a world and would go on to change the face of the universe. He had to recognize the possibility of death, for travel is always dangerous, and this more dangerous than most. But happiness is not something that can live in a cell.

Now the city was more silent than when he had come. What was it Morgan wrote? "The spires like gravestones." Tombs now for more than happiness.

Humanity had gone on a long roller coaster trip, but now the joy ride was over. It was a moment of gladness that Man would strive again and sadness that the dream, which proved too fair, was shattered. Like a birth and a wake.

"Is the Council dead?" Susan asked, beside him silently.

"Not yet. Dreaming, perhaps. Under sentence of death. The Council that made fantasies for others is now making fantasies for itself. It has a new law: Be happy! In obedience to that law, it has retreated within its own dream of paradise, forgetful of all else, too preoccupied to notice that it is dying.

"In time, insulation will rot, wires will short, electronic devices will fail, masonry will crack, steel will rust. But the rule of the God Hedon is over. As soon as it realized that it, too, must be happy, it was doomed. Because happiness is death."

"And now we must leave Earth. It seems a pity to leave so fair a world."

"Too fair—like the promise of happiness. Happiness must come from inside, or it is deadly. The only road for Man is the hard road, up and out—the road of dissatisfaction, the road of anger. The dreams are ended now in all the cells, in all the foster-wombs, all over the world, because the Council has forgotten them forever. Most of the embryos will die. But perhaps some —your father may be one—will survive the ordeal of being born again. The Council's automatic processes are keeping them alive, but when they are ready, they will break free. Let them have Earth. We have Venus and beyond. To look back is to die a little. To look forward is to live forever. Those who are worthy will eventually follow us."

One star was out. Like a brilliant beacon, it hung over the city.

"The Duplicates no longer walk the corridors of Morgan-town," Susan said, looking at the evening star. "Venus is safe. Humanity will live."

"Until the next crisis. For there is always another. I wonder how many of the colonists succumbed to the seductions of the Council's mechs. I would like to think that our hedonic society would have survived in any case, that enough of us could have resisted. But it would have been constant hell to have heaven always available for the asking."

"Yes." Susan looked steadily at D'glas for a moment. "How can we be sure—" she started to say, and then stopped.

"What is it?" D'glas asked.

"Nothing," she said. "I'll go get ready for the take-off."

She left him, without the backward glance that might have meant uncertainty. He stood there, not wondering what she had been about to say. He didn't have to wonder. He knew.

How could they be sure that this was reality, not another wish-fulfillment dream from the Council-mech? How could they be sure that they had really conquered it and were not just living an illusion in a watery cell?

The answer was: they could never be sure.

D'glas looked up into the night sky and shrugged. What did it matter? One god or another?

All a man had was himself and his faith in himself and such illusions as he chose to believe.

The rest was lies.

The Immortal

THE clinic was deserted.

Harry Elliott smothered a yawn as he walked slowly toward the draped operating table under the cold, glareless light at the back of the big room tiled in antiseptic white and flooded with invisible, germ-killing ultraviolet. He lit the candelabra of bunsen burners standing on each side of the table and turned on the ventilators under the mural of Immortality slaying Death with a hypodermic. The air, straight from the Medical Center, was pure, disease-free, and aromatic with the hospital incense of alcohol and ether.

Science, surgery, and salvation—the clinic had something for everybody.

It was going to be another ordinary day, Harry decided. Soon would come the shrill cacophony of six o'clock, and the factories would release their daily human floods into the worn channels between the high walls. For an hour or two, then, he would be busy.

But it was a good shift. He was busy only between six and curfew. Other times he could sneak a view of the *Geriatrics Journal* or flip a few reels of text over the inner surface of his glasses. He didn't need them for seeing—if he had he would have used contact lenses—but they were handy for viewing and they made a man look professional and older.

At eighteen that was important to Harry. . . .

Sunday was bad. But then Sunday was a bad day for everybody.

145

He would be glad when it was over. One more week and he would be back on duty inside. Six more months and he would have his residency requirements completed. As soon as he passed his boards—it was unthinkable that he would not pass—there would be no more clinics.

It was all very well to administer to the masses—that was what the oath of Hippocrates was about, partly—but a doctor had to be practical. There just wasn't enough medical care to go around. Curing an ear infection here, a case of gonorrhea there, was like pouring antibiotics into the river. The results were unnoticeable.

With those who had a chance at immortality, it was different. Saving a life meant something. It might even mean a reprieve for himself, when he needed it. And reprieves had been stretched into immortality.

The prognosis, though, was unfavorable. A man's best hope was to make something of himself worth saving. Then immortality would be voted him by a grateful electorate. That was why Harry had decided to specialize in geriatrics. Later, when he had more leisure and laboratory facilities, he would concentrate on the synthesis of the *elixir vitae*. Success would mean immortality not only for himself but for everybody. Even if he did not succeed within a lifetime, if his research was promising there would be reprieves.

But it was the synthesis that was important. The world could not continue to depend upon the Cartwrights. They were too selfish. They preferred to hide their own accidental immortality rather than contribute harmless amounts of blood at regular intervals. If Fordyce's statistical analysis of Locke's investigations were correct, there were enough Cartwrights alive to grant immortality to 50,000 mortals—and that number would increase geometrically as more Cartwrights were born. One day a baby would inherit life as its birthright, and not death.

If the Cartwrights were not so selfish . . . As it was, there had been only enough of them discovered to provide immortality for a hundred to two hundred persons; nobody knew exactly how many. And the tame Cartwrights were so infertile that their numbers increased very slowly. They could contribute only a limited quantity of the precious blood. From this could be extracted only a small amount of the gamma globulin that carried the immunity factor. Even at closely calculated minimal dosages, the shots could not be stretched beyond a small group of essential persons, because the immunity to death was passive. It was good for no more than thirty to forty days.

But once the blood protein was synthesized . . .

Harry had an idea of how it might be done—by taking apart the normal gamma globulin molecule and then putting it back together again, atom by atom. With radiation and the new quick freeze, absolute, he could do it. Once he got his hands on a research grant and laboratory facilities . . .

He walked slowly toward the street entrance, past the consultation rooms with their diagnostic couches on both sides of the long clinic hallway. He paused between the giant Aesculapian staffs that supported the lintel of the doorway, just before he reached the moving curtain of air that kept out the heat of summer, the cold of winter, and the dust and disease of the city. At this stage in his career, it was folly to think of research grants. They were for older, tried researchers, not for callow residents, nor even eager young specialists.

The clinic was built out from the Medical Center wall. Opposite was the high wall of a factory that made armored cars for export to the suburbs. That's where the Center got its ambulances. A little farther along the Medical Center wall was a second, smaller outbuilding. On its roof was a neon sign: BLOOD BOUGHT HERE. Beside its door would be another, smaller sign: "We Are Now Paying $5 a Pint."

In a few minutes the blood-bank technicians would be busy inserting needles into scarred antecubital veins as the laborers were set free by the quitting whistles. They would pour through the laboratory, spending their life resources prodigally, coming back, many of them, to give another pint before two weeks had elapsed, much less two months. No use trying to keep track of them. They would do anything: trade identity cards, scuff up their inner arms so that the previous needle hole would not show, swear that the scars were from antibiotic shots. . . .

And then they would gulp down their orange juice—some of the children did it mostly for that because they had never tasted orange juice before—grab their five dollars and head for the nearest shover of illicit antibiotics and nostrums. Or they would give it to some neighborhood leech for rubbing salve on some senile invalid or for chanting runes over some dying infant.

Well, they were essential. He had to remember that. They were a great pool of immunities. They had been exposed to all the diseases bred of poverty, ignorance, and filth from which the squires had been protected. The squires needed the citizens' gamma globulins, their antigens. The squires needed the serums manufactured in citizen bodies, the vaccines prepared from their reactions.

A remarkable teacher had once shocked him into awareness by saying: "Without filth there is no cleanliness; without disease there is no health." Harry remembered that in his contacts with the citizens. It helped.

Past the blood bank, the Center wall curved away. Beyond was the city. It was not dying; it was dead.

Wooden houses had subsided into heaps of rotten lumber. Brick tenements had crumbled; here and there a wall tottered against the sky. Aluminum and magnesium walls were dented and pierced. Decay was everywhere.

But, like green shoots pushing through the forest's mat of dead leaves, the city was being born again. A two-room shack was built with scavenged boards. A brick bungalow stood behind tenement ruins. Metal walls became rows of huts.

The eternal cycle, Harry thought. Out of death, life. Out of life, destruction. Only man could evade it.

All that remained of the original city were the walled factories and the vast hospital complexes. Behind their protective walls, they stood tall and strong and faceless. On the walls, armored guard houses glinted in the orange-red fire of the declining sun.

As Harry stood there, the whistles began to blow—all tones and volumes of them, making a strange, shrill counterpoint, suited to sunset in the city. It was primitive and stirring, like a savage ceremony to propitiate the gods and insure the sun's return.

The gates rolled up and left openings in the factory walls. Laborers spilled out into the street: all kinds of them, men and women, children and ancients, sickly and strong. Yet there was a sameness to them. They were ragged and dirty and diseased; they were the city dwellers.

They should have been miserable, but they were usually happy. They would look up at the blue sky, if the smog had not yet crept up from the river, and laugh, for no reason at all. The children would play tag between their parents' legs, yelling and giggling. Even the ancients would smile indulgently.

It was the healthy squires who were sober and concerned. Well, it was natural. Ignorance can be happy; the citizens need not be concerned about good health or immortality. It was beyond them. They could appear on a summer day like the May fly and flutter about gaily and die. But knowledge had to worry; immortality had its price.

Remembering that always made Harry feel better. Seeing the great hordes of citizens with no chance for immortality made him self-conscious about his advantages. He had been raised in a suburban villa far from the city's diseases and carcinogens. From infancy he had received the finest of medical care. He had been through four years of high school, eight years of medical school, and almost three years of residency training.

That gave him a head start toward immortality. It was right that he should pay for it with concern.

Where did they all come from? He thought: they must breed

like rabbits in those warrens. Where did they all go to? Back into the wreckage of the city, like the rats and the vermin.

He shuddered. Really, they were almost another race.

Tonight, though, they weren't laughing and singing. Even the children were silent. They marched down the street soberly, almost the only sound the tramp of their bare feet on the cracked pavement. Even the doors of the blood bank weren't busy.

Harry shrugged. Sometimes they were like this. The reason would be something absurd—a gang fight, company trouble, some dark religious rite that could never really be stamped out. Maybe it had something to do with the phases of the moon.

He went back into the clinic to get ready. The first patient was a young woman. She was an attractive creature with blond hair worn long around her shoulders and a ripe body—if you could ignore the dirt and the odor that drifted even into the professional chamber behind the consultation room.

He resisted an impulse to have her disrobe. Not because of any consequences—what was a citizen's chastity? A mythical thing like the unicorn. Besides, they expected it. From the stories the other doctors told, he thought they must come to the clinic for that purpose. But there was no use tempting himself. He would feel unclean for days.

She babbled as they always did. She had sinned against nature. She had not been getting enough sleep. She had not been taking her vitamins regularly. She had bought illicit terramycin from a shover for a kidney infection. It was all predictable and boring.

"I see," he kept muttering. And then, "I'm going to take a diagnosis now. Don't be frightened."

He switched on the diagnostic machine. A sphygmomanometer crept up snakelike from beneath the Freudian couch and encircled her arm. A mouthpiece slipped between her lips. A stethoscope counted her pulse. A skull cap fitted itself to her head. Metal caps slipped over her fingertips. Bracelets encircled her ankles. A band wrapped itself around her hips. The machine punctured, withdrew samples, counted, measured, listened, compared, correlated. . . .

In a moment it was over. Harry had his diagnosis. She was anemic; they all were. They couldn't resist that five dollars.

"Married?" he asked.

"Nah?" she said hesitantly.

"Better not waste any time. You're pregnant."

"Prag-nant?" she repeated.

"You're going to have a baby."

A joyful light broke across her face. "Aw! Is that all! I thought maybe it was a too-more. A baby I can take care of nicely. Tell me, doctor, will it be boy or girl?"

"A boy," Harry said wearily. *The slut!* Why did it always irritate him so?

She got up from the couch with a lithe, careless grace. "Thank you, doctor. I will go tell Georgie. He will be angry for a little, but I know how to make him glad."

There were others waiting in the consultation rooms, contemplating their symptoms. Harry checked the panel: a woman with pleurisy, a man with cancer, a child with rheumatic fever. . . . But Harry stepped out into the clinic to see if the girl dropped anything into the donation box as she passed. She didn't. Instead, she paused by the shover hawking his wares just outside the clinic door.

"Get your aureomycin here," he ranted, "your penicillin, your terramycin. A hypodermic with every purchase. Good health! Good health! Stop those sniffles before they lay you low, low, low. Don't let that infection cost you your job, your health, your life. Get your filters, your antiseptics, your vitamins. Get your amulets, your good-luck charms. I have here a radium needle which has already saved thirteen lives. And here is an ampule of *elixir vitae*. Get your ilotycin here. . . ."

The girl bought an amulet and hurried off to Georgie. A lump of anger burned in Harry's throat.

The throngs were still marching silently in the street. In the back of the clinic a woman was kneeling at the operating table. She took a vitamin pill and a paper cup of tonic from the dispensary.

Behind the walls the sirens started. Harry turned toward the doorway. The gate in the Medical Center wall rolled up.

First came the outriders on their motorcycles. The people in the street scattered to the walls on either side, leaving a lane down the center of the street. The outriders brushed carelessly close to them—healthy young squires, their nose filters in place, their goggled eyes haughty, their guns slung low on their hips.

That would have been something, Harry thought enviously—to have been a company policeman. There was a dash to them, a hint of violence. They were hell on wheels. And if they were one-tenth as successful with women as they were reputed to be, there was no woman—from citizen through technician and nurse up to their suburban peers—who was immune to them.

Well, let them have the glamor and the women. He had taken the safer and more certain route to immortality. Few company policemen made it.

After the outriders came an ambulance, its armored ports closed, its automatic 40-millimeter gun roaming restlessly for a target. More outriders covered the rear. Above the convoy a helicopter swooped low.

Something glinted in the sunlight, became a line of small round objects beneath the helicopter, dropping in an arc toward the street. One after another they broke with fragile, popping sounds. They strung up through the convoy.

Like puppets when the puppeteer has released the strings, the outriders toppled to the street, skidding limply as their motorcycles slowed and stopped on their single wheels.

The ambulance could not stop. It rolled over one of the fallen outriders and crashed into a motorcycle, bulldozing it out of the way. The 40-millimeter gun had jerked erratically to fix its radar sight on the helicopter, but the plane was skimming the rooftops. Before the gun could get the range the plane was gone.

Harry smelled something sharply penetrating. His head felt swollen and light. The street tilted and then straightened.

In the midst of the crowd beyond the ambulance an arm swung up. Something dark sailed through the air and smashed against the top of the ambulance. Flames splashed across it. They dripped down the sides, ran into gun slits and observation ports, were drawn into the air intake.

A moment followed in which nothing happened. The scene was like a frozen tableau—the ambulance and the motorcycles balanced in the street, the outriders and some of the nearest citizens crumpled and twisted on the pavement, the citizens watching, the flames licking up toward greasy, black smoke. . . .

The side door of the ambulance fell open. A medic staggered out, clutching something in one hand, beating at flames on his white jacket with the other.

The citizens watched silently, not moving to help or hinder. From among them stepped a dark-haired man. His hand went up. It held something limp and dark. The hand came down against the medic's head.

No sound came to Harry over the roar of the idling motorcycles and ambulance. The pantomime continued, and he was part of the frozen audience as the medic fell and the man stooped, patted out the flames with his bare hands, picked the object out of the medic's hand, and looked at the ambulance door.

There was a girl standing there, Harry noticed. From this distance Harry could tell little more than that she was dark-haired and slender.

The flames on the ambulance had burnt themselves out. The girl stood in the doorway, not moving. The man beside the fallen medic looked at her, started to hold out a hand, stopped, let it drop, turned, and faded back into the crowd.

Less than two minutes had passed since the sirens began.

Silently the citizens pressed forward. The girl turned and went back into the ambulance. The citizens stripped the outriders of their clothing and weapons, looted the ambulance of its black bag and medical supplies, picked up their fallen fellows, and disappeared.

It was like magic. One moment the street was full of them. The next moment they were gone. The street was empty of life.

Behind the Medical Center walls the sirens began again.

It was like a release. Harry began running down the street, his throat swelling with shouts. There were no words to them.

Out of the ambulance came a young boy. He was slim and small —no more than seven years old. He had blond hair, cut very short, and dark eyes in a tanned face. He wore a ragged T-shirt that once might have been white and a pair of blue jeans cut off above the knees.

He reached an arm back into the ambulance. A yellowed claw came out to meet it, and then an arm. The arm was a gnarled stick encircled with ropy blue veins like lianas. It was attached to a man on stiff, stiltlike legs. He was very old. His hair was thin, white silk. His scalp and face were wrinkled parchment. A tattered tunic fell from bony shoulders, around his permanently bent back, and was caught in folds around his loins.

The boy led the old man slowly and carefully into the ruined street, because the man was blind, his eyelids flat and dark over empty sockets. The old man bent painfully over the fallen medic. His fingers explored the medic's skull. Then he moved to the outrider who had been run over by the ambulance. The man's chest was crushed; a pink froth edged his lips as punctured lungs gasped for breath.

He was as good as dead. Medical science could do nothing for injuries that severe, that extensive.

Harry reached the old man, seized him by one bony shoulder. "What do you think you're doing?" he asked.

The old man didn't move. He held to the outrider's hand for a moment and then creaked to his feet. "Healing," he answered in a voice like the whisper of sandpaper.

"That man's dying," Harry said.

"So are we all," said the old man.

Harry glanced down at the outrider. Was he breathing easier, or was that illusion?

It was then the stretcher bearers reached them.

Harry had a difficult time finding the Dean's office. The Medical Center covered hundreds of city blocks, and it had grown under a strange stimulus of its own. No one had ever planned for it to be so big, but it had sprouted an arm here when demand for medical care and research outgrew the space available, a wing there, and arteries through and under and around. . . .

He followed the glowing guidestick through the unmarked corridors, and tried to remember the way. But it was useless. He inserted the stick into the lock on an armored door. The door swallowed the stick and opened. As soon as Harry had entered, the door swung shut and locked. He was in a bare anteroom. On a metal bench bolted to the floor along one wall sat the boy and the old man from the ambulance. The boy looked up at Harry curiously and then his gaze returned to his folded hands. The old man rested against the wall.

A little farther along the bench was a girl. She looked like the girl who had stood in the doorway of the ambulance, but she was smaller than he had thought and younger. Her face was pale. Only her blue eyes were vivid as they looked at him with a curious appeal and then faded. His gaze dropped to her figure; it was boyish and unformed, clad in a simple brown dress belted at the waist. She was no more than twelve or thirteen years old, he thought.

The reception box had to repeat the question twice: "Name?"

"Dr. Harry Elliott," he said.

"Advance for confirmation."

He went to the wall beside the far door and put his right hand against the plate set into it. A light flashed into his right eye, comparing retinal patterns.

"Deposit all metal objects in the receptable," the box said.

Harry hesitated, and then pulled his stethoscope out of his jacket pocket, removed his watch, emptied his trouser pockets of coins and pocketknife and hypospray.

Something clicked. "Nose filters," the box said.

Harry put those into the receptable, too. The girl was watching him, but when he looked at her, her eyes moved away. The door opened. He went through the doorway. The door closed behind him.

Dean Mock's office was a magnificent room, thirty feet long and twenty feet wide. It was decorated in mid-Victorian style. The furniture all looked like real antiques, especially the yellow-oak rolltop desk and the mahogany instrument cabinet.

The room looked rich and impressive. Personally, though, Harry preferred Twentieth Century Modern. Its clean chromium-and-glass lines were esthetically pleasing; moreover, they were from the respectable first days of medical science—that period when mankind first began to realize that good health was not merely an accident, that it could be bought if men were willing to pay the price.

Harry had seen Dean Mock before, but never to speak to. His parents couldn't understand that. They thought he was the peer of everyone in the Medical Center because he was a doctor. He kept telling them how big the place was, how many people it contained: 75,000, 100,000—only the statisticians knew how many. It didn't do any good; they still couldn't understand. Harry had given up trying.

The Dean didn't know Harry. He sat behind the rolltop desk in his white jacket and studied Harry's record cast up on the frosted glass insert. He was good at it but you couldn't deceive a man who had studied like that for ten years in this Center alone.

The Dean's black hair was thinning. He was almost eighty years old now, but he didn't look it. He came of good stock, and he had had the best of medical care. He was good for another twenty years, Harry estimated, without longevity shots. By that time, surely, with his position and his accomplishments, he would be voted a reprieve.

Once, when a bomb had exploded in the power room, some of the doctors had whispered in the safe darkness that Mock's youthful appearance had a more reasonable explanation than heredity, but they were wrong. Harry had searched the lists, and Mock's name wasn't on them.

Mock looked up quickly and caught Harry staring at him. Harry glanced away, but not before he had seen in Mock's eyes a look of—what?—fright? desperation?

Harry couldn't understand it. The raid had been daring, this close to the Center walls, but nothing new. There had been raids before; there would be raids again. Any time there is something valuable, lawless men will try to steal it. In Harry's day it happened to be medicine.

Mock said abruptly, "Then you saw the man? You could recognize him if you saw him again, or if you had a good solidograph?"

"Yes, sir," Harry said. Why was Mock making such a production out of it? He had already been over this with the head resident and the chief of the company police.

"Do you know Governor Weaver?" Mock asked.

"An Immortal!"

"No, no," Mock said impatiently. "Do you know where he lives?"

"In the Governor's mansion. Forty miles from here, almost due west."

"Yes, yes," Mock said. "You're going to carry a message to him, a message. The shipment has been hijacked. Hijacked." Mock had a nervous habit of repeating words. Harry had to listen intently to keep from being distracted. "It will be a week before another shipment is ready, a week. How we will get it to him I don't know. I don't know." The last statement was muttered to himself.

Harry tried to make sense out of it. Carry a message to the Governor? "Why don't you call him?" he said, unthinking.

But the question only roused Mock out of his introspection. "The underground cables are cut. Cut. No use repairing them. Repair men get shot. And even if they're fixed, they're only cut again next night. Radio and television are jammed. Get ready. You'll have to hurry to get out the southwest gate before curfew."

"A pass will get me through," Harry said, uncomprehending. Was Mock going insane?

"Didn't I tell you? Tell you?" Mock passed the back of his hand across his forehead as if to clear away cobwebs. "You're going alone, on foot, dressed as a citizen. A convoy would be cut to pieces. To pieces. We've tried. We've been out of touch with the Governor for three weeks. Three weeks! He must be getting impatient. Never make the Governor impatient. It isn't healthy."

For the first time Harry really understood what the Dean was asking him to do. The Governor! He had it in his power to cut half a lifetime off Harry's personal quest for immortality. "But my residency—"

Mock looked wise. "The Governor can do you more good than a dozen boards. More good."

Harry caught his lower lip between his teeth and counted off on his fingers. "I'll need nose filters, a small medical kit, a gun—"

Mock was shaking his head. "None of those. Out of character. If you reach the Governor's mansion, it will be because you pass as a citizen, not because you defend yourself well or heal up your wounds afterward. And a day or two without filters won't reduce your life expectancy appreciably. Well, doctor? Will you get through?"

"As I hope for immortality!" Harry said earnestly.

"Good, good. One more thing. You'll take along with you the people you saw in the anteroom. The boy's name is Christopher; the old man calls himself Pearce. He's some kind of neighborhood leech. The Governor has asked for him."

"A leech?" Harry said incredulously.

Mock shrugged. His expression said that he considered the exclamation impertinent, but Harry could not restrain himself, and he said, "If we made an example of a few of these quacks—"

"The clinics would be more crowded than they are now. Now. They serve a good purpose. Besides, what can we do? He doesn't claim to be a physician. He calls himself a healer. He doesn't drug, operate, advise, or manipulate. Sick people come to him and he touches them. Touches them. Is that practicing medicine?"

Harry shook his head.

"What if the sick people claim to be helped? Pearce claims nothing. Nothing. He charges nothing. Nothing. If the sick people are grateful, if they want to give him something, who is to stop them?"

Harry sighed. "I'll have to sleep. They'll get away."

Mock jeered, "A feeble old man and a boy?"

"The girl's lively enough."

"Marna?" Mock reached into a drawer and brought out a hinged silver circle. He tossed it to Harry. Harry caught it and looked at it.

"It's a bracelet. Put it on."

It looked like nothing more than a bracelet. Harry shrugged, slipped it over his wrist, and clamped it shut. For a moment it seemed too big, and then it tightened. His wrist tingled where the bracelet touched him.

"It's tuned to the one on the girl's wrist. Tuned. When the girl moves away from you, her wrist will tingle. The farther she goes, the more it will hurt. After a little she will come back. I'd put bracelets on the boy and the old man, but they only work in pairs. Pairs. If someone tries to remove the bracelet forcibly, the girl will die. Die. It links itself to the nervous system. The Governor has the only key."

Harry stared at Mock. "What about mine?"

"The same. For you it's a warning device."

Harry took a deep breath and looked down at his wrist. The silver gleamed now like a snake's flat eyes.

"Why didn't you have one on the medic?"

"We did. We had to amputate his arm to get it off." Mock turned to his desk and started the microfilmed reports flipping past the window again. In a moment he looked up and seemed startled that Harry had not moved. "Still here? Get started. Wasted too much time now if you're going to beat curfew."

Harry turned and started toward the door through which he had come.

"Watch out for ghouls," Dean Mock called after him. "And mind the head-hunters."

By the time they reached the southwest gate, Harry had evolved a method of progress for his little group that was mutually unsatisfactory.

"Hurry up," he would say. "There's only a few minutes left before curfew."

The girl would look at him and look away. Pearce, already moving more rapidly than Harry had expected, would say, "Patience. We'll get there."

None of them would speed up. Harry would walk ahead rapidly, outdistancing the others. His wrist would begin to tingle, then to smart, to burn, and to hurt. The farther he left Marna behind, the worse his pain grew. Only the thought that her wrist felt just as bad sustained him.

After a little the pain would begin to ebb. He knew then, without looking, that she had broken. When he would turn, she would be twenty feet behind him, no closer, willing to accept that much pain to keep from coming nearer to him.

Then he would have to stop and wait for the old man. Once she walked on past, but after a little she could stand the pain no more, and she returned. After that she stopped when he did.

It was a small triumph for Harry, but something to strengthen him when he started thinking about the deadly thing on his wrist and the peculiar state of the world, in which the Medical Center had been out of touch with the Governor's mansion for three weeks, in which a convoy could not get through, in which a message had to be sent by a foot messenger.

Under other conditions, Harry might have thought Marna a lovely thing. She was slim and graceful, her skin was clear, her features were regular and pleasing, and the contrast between her dark hair and her blue eyes was striking. But she was young and spiteful and linked to him by a hateful condition. They had been thrown together too intimately too soon; and, besides, she was only a child.

They reached the gate with only a minute to spare.

On either side of them the chain-link double fence stretched as far as Harry could see. There was no end to it, really; it completely encircled the town. At night it was electrified, and savage dogs roamed the space between the fences.

Somehow citizens still got out. They formed outlaw bands that attacked defenseless travelers. That would be one of the dangers.

The head guard at the gate was a dark-skinned, middle-aged squire. At sixty he had given up any hopes for immortality; he intended to get what he could out of this life. That included bullying his inferiors.

He looked at the blue, daylight-only pass, and then at Harry. "Topeka? On foot." He chuckled. It made his big belly shake until he had to cough. "If the ghouls don't get you, the head-hunters will. The bounty on heads is twenty dollars now. Outlaw heads only—but then, heads don't talk. Not if they're detached from bodies. Of course, that's what you're figuring on doing—joining a wolf pack." He spat on the sidewalk beside Harry's foot.

Harry jerked back his foot in revulsion. The guard's eyes brightened.

"Are you going to let us through?" Harry asked.

"Let you through?" Slowly the guard looked at his wrist watch. "Can't do that. Past curfew. See?"

Automatically Harry bent over to look. "But we got here before curfew—" he began. The guard's fist hit him just above the left ear and sent him spinning away.

"Get back in there and stay in there, you filthy citizens!" the guard shouted.

Harry's hand went to his pocket where he kept the hypospray, but it was gone. Words that would blast the guard off his post and into oblivion trembled on his lips, but he dared not utter them. He wasn't Dr. Elliott any more, not until he reached the Governor's mansion. He was Harry Elliott, citizen, fair game for any man's fist, who should consider himself lucky it was only a fist.

"Now," the guard said suggestively, "if you were to leave the girl as security—" He coughed.

Marna shrank back. She touched Harry accidentally. It was the first time they had touched, in spite of a more intimate linkage that joined them in pain and release, and something happened to Harry. His body recoiled automatically from the touch, as it would from a scalding sterilizer. Marna stiffened, aware of him.

Harry, disturbed, saw Pearce shuffling toward the guard, guided by his voice. Pearce reached out, his hand searching. He touched the guard's tunic, then his arm, and worked his way down the arm to the hand. Harry stood still, his hand doubled into a fist at his side, waiting for the guard to hit the old man. But the guard gave Pearce the instinctive respect due age and only looked at him curiously.

"Weak lungs," Pearce whispered. "Watch them. Pneumonia might kill before antibiotics could help. And in the lower left lobe, a hint of cancer—"

"Aw, now!" The guard jerked his hand away, but his voice was frightened.

"X-ray," Pearce whispered. "Don't wait."

"There—there ain't nothing wrong with me," the guard stammered. "You—you're trying to scare me." He coughed.

"No exertion. Sit down. Rest."

"Why, I'll—I'll—" He began coughing violently. He jerked his head at the gate. "Go on," he said, choking. "Go out there and die."

The boy Christopher took the old man's hand and led him through the open gateway. Harry caught Marna's upper arm—again the contact—and half helped her, half pushed her through the gate, keeping his eye warily on the guard. But the man's eyes were turned inward toward something far more vital to himself.

As soon as they were through, the gate slammed down behind them and Harry released Marna's arm as if it were distasteful to hold it. Fifty yards beyond, down the right-hand lanes of the disused six-lane divided highway, Harry said, "I suppose I ought to thank you."

Pearce whispered, "That would be polite."

Harry rubbed his head where the guard had hit him. It was swelling. He wished for a medical kit. "How can I be polite to a charlatan?"

"Politeness does not cost."

"Still—to lie to the man about his condition. To say—cancer—" Harry had a hard time saying it. It was a bad word—it was the one disease, aside from death itself, for which medical science had found no final cure.

"Was I lying?"

Harry stared sharply at the old man and then shrugged. He looked at Marna. "We're all in this together. We might as well make it as painless as possible. If we try to get along together, we might even all make it alive."

"Get along?" Marna said. Harry heard her speak for the first time; her voice was low and melodious, even in anger. "With this?" She held up her arm. The silver bracelet gleamed in the last red rays of the sun.

Harry said harshly, raising his wrist, "You think it's any better for me?"

Pearce whispered, "We will cooperate, Christopher and I—I, Dr. Elliott, because I am too old to do anything else, and Christopher because he is young and discipline is good for the young."

Christopher grinned. "Grampa used to be a doctor before he learned how to be a healer."

"Pride dulls the senses and warps the judgment," Pearce said softly.

Harry held back a comment. Now was no time to argue about medicine and quackery.

The road was deserted. The once magnificent pavement was cracked and broken. Grass sprouted tall and thick in the cracks. The weeds stood like young trees along both edges, here and there the big, brown faces of sunflowers, fringed in yellow, nodding peacefully.

Beyond were the ruins of what had once been called the suburbs. The distinction between them and the city had been only a line drawn on a map; there had been no fences then. When they had gone up, the houses outside had soon crumbled.

The real suburbs were far out. First it was turnpike time to the city that had become more important than distance; then helicopter time. Finally time had run out for the city. It had become so obviously a sea of carcinogens and disease that the connection to the suburbs had been broken. Shipments of food and raw materials went in and shipments of finished materials came out, but nobody went there any more—except to the medical centers. They were located in the cities because their raw material was there: the blood, the organs, the diseases, the bodies for experiment. . . .

Harry walked beside Marna, ahead of Christopher and Pearce, but the girl didn't look at him. She walked on, her eyes straight ahead, as if she were alone. Harry said finally, "Look, it's not my fault. I didn't ask for this. Can't we be friends?"

She glanced at him just once. "No!"

His lips tightened, and he dropped away. He let his wrist tingle. What did he care if a thirteen-year-old girl disliked him?

The western sky was fading from scarlet into lavender and purple. Nothing moved in the ruins or along the road. They were alone in an ocean of desolation. They might have been the last people on a ruined earth.

Harry shivered. Soon it would be hard to keep to the road. "Hurry," he said to Pearce, "if you don't want to spend the night out here with the ghouls and the head-hunters."

"There are worse companions," Pearce whispered.

By the time they reached the motel, the moonless night was completely upon them and the old suburbs were behind. The sprawling place was dark except for a big neon sign that said "MOTEL," a smaller sign that said "Vacancy," and, at the gate in the fence that surrounded the whole place, a mat that said "Welcome." On a frosted glass plate were the words, "Push button."

Harry was about to push the button when Christopher said urgently, "Dr. Elliott, look!" He pointed toward the fence at the right with a stick he had picked up half a mile back.

"What?" Harry snapped. He was tired and nervous and dirty. He peered into the darkness. "A dead rabbit."

"Christopher means the fence is electrified," Marna said, "and the mat you're standing on is made of metal. I don't think we should go in here."

"Nonsense!" Harry said sharply. "Would you rather stay out here at the mercy of whatever roams the night? I've stopped at these motels before. There's nothing wrong with them."

Christopher held out his stick. "Maybe you'd better push the button with this."

Harry frowned, took the stick, and stepped off the mat. "Oh, all right," he said ungraciously. At the second try, he pushed the button.

The frosted glass plate became a television eye. "Who rings?"

"Four travelers bound for Topeka," Harry said. He held up the pass in front of the eye. "We can pay."

"Welcome," said the speaker. "Cabins thirteen and fourteen will open when you deposit the correct amount of money. What time do you wish to be awakened?"

Harry looked at his companions. "Sunrise," he said.

"Good night," said the speaker. "Sleep tight."

The gate rolled up. Christopher led Pearce around the welcome mat and down the driveway beyond. Marna followed. Irritated, Harry jumped over the mat and caught up with them.

A single line of glass bricks along the edge of the driveway glowed fluorescently to point out the way they should go. They passed a tank trap and several machine-gun emplacements, but the place was deserted.

When they reached cabin 13, Harry said, "We won't need the other one; we'll stay together." He put three twenty-dollar uranium pieces into the coin slot.

"Thank you," the door said. "Come in."

As the door opened, Christopher darted inside. The small room held a double bed, a chair, a desk, and a floor lamp. In the corner was a small partitioned bathroom with an enclosed shower, a lavatory, and a toilet. The boy went immediately to the desk, removed a plastic menu card from it, and returned to the door. He helped Pearce enter the room and then waited by the door until Harry and Marna were inside. He cracked the menu card into two pieces. As the door swung shut, he slipped one of the pieces between the door and the jamb. As he started back toward Pearce, he stumbled against the lamp and knocked it over. It crashed and went out. They were left with only the illumination from the bathroom light.

"Clumsy little fool!" Harry said.

Marna was at the desk, writing. She turned and handed the paper to Harry. He edged toward the light and looked at it. It said:

Christopher has broken the eye, but the room is still bugged. We can't break that without too much suspicion. Can I speak to you outside?

"That is the most ridiculous—" Harry began.

"This seems adequate," Pearce whispered. "You two can sleep in fourteen." His blind face was turned intently toward Harry.

Harry sighed. He might as well humor them. He opened the door and stepped into the night with Marna. The girl moved close to him, put her arms around his neck and her cheek against his. Without his volition, his arms went around her waist. Her lips moved against his ear; a moment later he realized that she was speaking.

"I do not like you, Dr. Elliott, but I do not want us all killed. Can you afford another cabin?"

"Of course, but—I'm not going to leave those two alone."

"It would be foolish for us not to stick together. Please, now. Ask no questions. When we go in fourteen, take off your jacket and throw it casually over the lamp. I'll do the rest."

Harry let himself be led to the next cabin. He fed the door. It greeted them and let them in. The room was identical with 13. Marna slipped a piece of plastic between the door and the jamb as the door closed. She looked at Harry expectantly.

He shrugged, took off his jacket, and tossed it over the lamp. The room took on a shadowy and sinister appearance. Marna knelt, rolled up a throw rug, and pulled down the covers on the bed. She went to the wall phone, gave it a little tug, and the entire flat vision plate swung out on hinges. She reached into it, grabbed something, and pulled it out. There seemed to be hundreds of turns of copper wire on a spool.

Marna went to the shower enclosure, unwinding wire as she went. She stood outside the enclosure and fastened one end of the wire to the hot-water faucet. Then she strung it around the room like a spider's web, broke it off, and fastened the end to the drain in the shower floor. She threaded the second piece of wire through the room close to but not touching the first wire.

Careful not to touch the wires, she reached into the shower enclosure and turned on the hot-water faucet. It gurgled, but no hot water came out. She tiptoed her way out between the wires, picked up the throw rug, and tossed it on the bed.

"Well, 'night," she said, motioning Harry toward the door and gesturing for him to be careful of the wires. When Harry reached the door without mishap, Marna turned off the lamp and removed the jacket.

She let the door slam behind them and gave a big sigh of relief.

"Now you've fixed it!" Harry whispered savagely. "I can't take a shower, and I'll have to sleep on the floor."

"You wouldn't want to take a shower anyway," Marna said. "It would be your last one. All of them are wired. You can have the bed if you want it, although I'd advise you to sleep on the floor with the rest of us."

Harry couldn't sleep. First it had been the room, shadowed and silent, and then the harsh breathing of the old man and the softer breaths of Christopher and Marna. As a resident, he was not used to sleeping in the same room with other persons.

Then his arm had tingled—not much, but just enough to keep him awake. He had got out of bed and crawled to where Marna was lying on the floor. She, too, had been awake. Silently he had urged her to share the bed with him, gesturing that he would not touch her. He had no desire to touch her, and if he had, he swore by Hippocrates that he would restrain himself. He only wanted to ease the tingling under the bracelet so that he could go to sleep.

She motioned that he could lie on the floor beside her, but he shook his head. Finally she relented enough to move to the floor beside the bed. By lying on his stomach and letting his arm dangle, Harry relieved the tingling and fell into an uneasy sleep.

He had dreams. There was one in which he was performing a long and difficult lung resection. The microsurgical controls slipped in his sweaty fingers; the scalpel sliced through the aorta. The patient started up on the operating table, the blood spurting from her heart. It was Marna. She began to chase him down long, hospital halls.

The overhead lights kept getting farther and farther apart until Harry was running in complete darkness through warm, sticky blood that rose higher and higher until it closed over his head.

Harry woke up, smothering, fighting against something that enveloped him completely, relentlessly. There was a sound of scuffling nearby. Something spat and crackled. Someone cursed.

Harry fought, futilely. Something ripped. Again. Harry caught a glimpse of a grayer darkness, struggled toward it, and came out through a long rip in the taut blanket, which had been pulled under the bed on all four sides.

"Quick!" Christopher said, folding up his pocketknife. He headed for the door where Pearce was already standing patiently.

Marna picked up a metal leg which had been unscrewed from the desk. Christopher slipped the chair out from under the door knob and silently opened the door. He led Pearce outside, and Marna followed. Dazedly, Harry came after her.

In cabin 14 someone screamed. Something flashed blue. A body fell. Harry smelled the odor of burning flesh.

Marna ran ahead of them toward the gate. She rested the ferule of the desk leg on the ground and let the metal bar fall toward the fence. The fence spat blue flame, which ran, crackling, down the desk leg. The leg glowed redly and sagged. Then everything went dark, including the neon sign above them and the light at the gate.

"Help me!" Marna panted.

She was trying to lift the gate. Harry put his hands underneath and lifted. The gate moved a foot and stuck.

Up the drive someone yelled hoarsely, without words. Harry strained at the gate. It yielded, rolled up silently. He put up his hand to hold it up while Marna got through, and then Pearce and the boy. Harry edged under and let the gate drop.

A moment later the electricity flickered on again. The desk leg melted through and dropped away.

Harry looked back. Coming toward them was a motorized wheelchair. In it was something lumpy and monstrous, a nightmarish menace—until Harry recognized it for what it was: a basket case, a quadruple amputee complicated by a heart condition. An artificial heart-and-lung machine rode on the back of the wheelchair like a second head. Behind galloped a gangling scarecrow creature with hair that flowed out behind. It wore a dress in imitation of a woman. . . .

Harry stood there watching, fascinated, while the wheelchair stopped beside one of the gun emplacements. Wires reached out from one of the chair arms like Medusan snakes, inserted themselves into control plugs. The machine gun started to chatter. Something plucked at Harry's sleeve.

The spell was broken. He turned and ran into the darkness.

Half an hour later he was lost. Marna, Pearce, and the boy were gone. All he had left was a tired body, an arm that burned, and a wrist that hurt worse than anything he could remember.

He felt his upper arm. His sleeve was wet. He brought his fingers to his nose. Blood. The bullet had creased him.

He sat disconsolately on the edge of the turnpike, the darkness as thick as soot around him. He looked at the fluorescent dial of his watch. Three-twenty. A couple of hours until sunrise. He sighed and tried to ease the pain in his wrist by rubbing around the bracelet. It seemed to help. In a few minutes it dropped to a tingle.

"Dr. Elliott," someone said softly.

He turned. Relief and something like joy flooded through his chest. There, outlined against the dim starlight, were Christopher, Marna, and Pearce.

"Well," Harry said gruffly, "I'm glad you didn't try to escape."

"We wouldn't do that, Dr. Elliott," Christopher said.

"How did you find me?" Harry asked.

Marna silently held up her arm.

The bracelet. Of course. He had given them too much credit, Harry thought sourly. Marna sought him out because she could not help herself, and Christopher, because he was out here alone with a senile old man to take care of and he needed help.

Although, honesty forced him to admit, it had been himself and not Christopher and Pearce who had needed help back there a mile or two. If they had depended on him, their heads would be drying in the motel's dry-storage room, waiting to be turned in for the bounty. Or their still-living bodies would be on their way to some organ bank somewhere.

"Christopher," Harry said to Pearce, "must have been apprenticed to a bad-debt evader."

Pearce accepted it for what it was: a compliment and an apology. "Dodging the collection agency traps and keeping out of the way of the health inspector," he whispered, "make growing up in the city a practical education. . . . You're hurt."

Harry started. How did the old man know? Even with eyes, it was too dark to see more than silhouettes. Harry steadied himself. It was an instinct, perhaps. Diagnosticians got it, sometimes, he was told, after they had been practicing for years. They could smell disease before the patient lay down on the couch. From the gauges they got only confirmation.

Or maybe it was simpler than that. Maybe the old man smelled the blood with a nose grown keen to compensate for his blindness.

The old man's fingers were on his arm, surprisingly gentle. Harry pulled his arm away roughly. "It's only a crease."

Pearce's fingers found his arm again. "It's bleeding. Find some dry grass, Christopher."

Marna was close. She had made a small, startled movement toward him when Pearce had discovered his wound. Harry could not accept her actions for sympathy; her hate was too tangible. Perhaps she was wondering what she would do if he were to die.

Pearce ripped the sleeve away.

"Here's the grass, Grampa," Christopher said.

How did the boy find dry grass in the dark? "You aren't going to put that on the wound!" Harry said quickly.

"It will stop the bleeding," Pearce whispered.

"But the germs—"

"Germs can't hurt you—unless you want them to."

He put the grass on the wound and bound it with the sleeve. "That will be better soon."

He would take it off, Harry told himself, as soon as they started walking. Somehow, though, it was easier to let it alone now that the harm was done. After that he forgot about it.

When they were walking again, Harry found himself beside Marna. "I suppose you got your education dodging health inspectors in the city, too?" he said drily.

She shook her head. "No. There's never been much else to do. Ever since I can remember I've been trying to escape. I got free once." Her voice was filled with remembered happiness. "I was free for twenty-four hours, and then they found me."

"But I thought—" Harry began. "Who are you?"

"Me? I'm the Governor's daughter."

Harry recoiled. It was not so much the fact, but the bitterness with which she spoke that impressed him.

Sunrise found them on the turnpike. They had passed the last ruined motel. Now, on either side of the turnpike, were rolling, grassy hills, valleys filled with trees, and the river winding muddily beside them, sometimes so close they could have thrown a stone into it, sometimes turning beyond the hills out of sight.

The day was warm. Above them the sky was blue, with only a trace of fleecy cloud on the western horizon. Occasionally a rabbit would hop across the road in front of them and vanish into the brush on the other side. Once they saw a deer lift its head beside the river and stare at them curiously.

Harry stared back with hunger in his eyes.

"Dr. Elliott," Christopher said.

Harry looked at him. In the boy's soiled hand was an irregular lump of solidified brown sugar. It was speckled with lint and other unidentifiable additions, but at the moment it was the most desirable object Harry could think of. His mouth watered, and he swallowed hard. "Give it to Pearce and the girl. They'll need their strength. And you, too."

"That's all right," Christopher said. "I have more." He held up three other pieces in his other hand. He gave one to Marna and one to Pearce. The old man bit into his with the stubs that served him as teeth.

Harry picked off the largest pieces of foreign matter, and then could restrain his hunger no longer. It was an unusually satisfying breakfast.

They kept walking, not moving rapidly but steadily. Pearce never complained. He kept his bent old legs tottering forward, and Harry gave up trying to move him faster.

They passed a hydroponic farm with an automated canning factory close beside it. No one moved around either building. Only the belts turned, carrying the tanks toward the factory to be harvested, or away from it refilled with nutrients, replanted with new crops.

"We should get something for lunch," Harry said. It would be theft, but it would be in a good cause. He could get his pardon directly from the Governor.

"Too dangerous," Christopher said.

"Every possible entrance," Marna said, "is guarded by spy beams and automatic weapons."

"Christopher will get us a good supper," Pearce whispered.

They saw a suburban villa on a distant hill, but there was no one in sight around it. They plodded on along the grass-grown double highway toward Lawrence.

Suddenly Christopher said, "Down! In the ditch beside the road!"

This time Harry moved quickly, without questions. He helped Pearce down the slope—the old man was very light—and threw himself down into the ditch beside Marna. A minute later they heard motors race by not far away. After they passed, Harry risked a glance above the top of the ditch. A group of motorcycles dwindled on the road toward the city. "What was that?" Harry asked, shaken.

"Wolf pack!" Marna said, hatred and disgust mingled in her voice.

"But they looked like company police," Harry said.

"When they grow up they will be company policemen," Marna said.

"I thought the wolf packs were made up of escaped citizens," Harry said.

Marna looked at him scornfully. "Is that what they tell you?"

"A citizen," Pearce whispered, "is lucky to stay alive when he's alone. A group of them wouldn't last a week."

They got back up on the turnpike and started walking again. Christopher was nervous as he led Pearce. He kept turning to look behind them and glancing from side to side. Soon Harry was edgy too.

"Down!" Christopher shouted.

Something whistled a moment before Harry was struck a solid blow in the middle of the back as he was throwing himself to the pavement. It knocked him hard to the ground. Marna screamed.

Harry rolled over, wondering if his back was broken. Christopher and Pearce were on the pavement beside him, but Marna was gone.

A rocket blasted a little ahead and above them. Then another.

Pearce looked up. A powered glider zoomed toward the sky. Marna was dangling from it, her body twisting and struggling to get free. From a second glider swung empty talons—padded hooks which had closed around Marna and had almost swooped up Harry.

Harry got to his knees, clutching his wrist. It was beginning to send stabs of pain up his arms, like a prelude to a symphony of anguish. The only thing that kept him from falling to the pavement in writhing torment was the black anger that surged through his veins and fought off weakness. He shook his fist at the turning gliders, climbing on smoking jets.

"Dr. Elliott!" Christopher said urgently.

Harry looked toward the voice with blurred eyes. The boy was in the ditch again. So was the old man.

"They'll be back! Get down!" Christopher said.

"But they've got Marna!" Harry said.

"It won't help if you get killed."

One glider swooped like a hawk toward a mouse. The other, carrying Marna, continued to circle as it climbed. Harry rolled toward the ditch. A line of chattering bullets chipped at the pavement where he had been.

"I thought," he gasped, "they were trying to abduct us."

"They hunt heads, too," Christopher said.

"Anything for a thrill," Pearce whispered.

"I never did anything like that," Harry moaned. "I never knew anyone who did."

"You were busy," Pearce said.

It was true. Since he was four years old he had been in school constantly, the last part of tht time in medical school. He had been home only for a brief day now and then; he scarcely knew his parents any more. What would he know of the pastimes of young squires? But this—this wolf-pack business! It was a degradation of life that filled him with horror.

The first glider was now a small cross in the sky; Marna, a speck hanging from it. It straightened and glided toward Lawrence. The second followed.

Suddenly Harry began beating the ground with his aching arm. "Why did I dodge? I should have let myself be captured with her. She'll die."

"She's strong," Pearce whispered, "stronger than you or Christopher, stronger than almost anyone. But sometimes strength is the cruelest thing. Follow her. Get her away."

Harry looked at the bracelet from which pain lanced up his arm and through his body. Yes, he could follow her. As long as he could move, he could find her. But feet were so slow against glider wings.

"The motorcycles will be coming back," Christopher said. "The gliders will have radioed them."

"But how do we capture a motorcycle?" Harry asked. The pain wouldn't let him think clearly.

Christopher had already pulled up his T-shirt. Around his thin waist was wrapped turn after turn of nylon cord. "Sometimes we fish," he said. He stretched the cord across the two-lane pavement in the concealment of grass grown tall in a crack. He motioned Harry to lie flat on the other side. "Let them pass, all but the last one," he said. "Hope that he's a straggler, far enough behind so that the others won't notice when we stand up. Wrap the cord around your waist. Get it up where it will catch him around the chest."

Harry lay beside the pavement. His left arm felt like a swelling balloon, and the balloon was filled with pain. He looked at it once, curiously, but it was still the same size.

After an eternity came the sound of motors, many of them. As the first ones passed, Harry cautiously lifted his head. Yes, there was a straggler. He was about a hundred feet behind the others; he was speeding now to catch up.

The others passed. When the straggler got within twenty feet Harry jumped up, bracing himself against the impact. Christopher sprang up at the same instant. The young squire had time only to look surprised before he hit the cord. The cord pulled Harry out into the middle of the pavement, his heels skidding. Christopher had tied his end to the trunk of a young tree.

The squire smashed into the pavement. The motorcycle slowed and stopped. Beyond, far down the road, the others had not looked back.

Harry untangled himself from the cord and ran to the squire. He was about as old as Harry, and as big. He had a harelip and a withered leg. He was dead. The skull was crushed.

Harry closed his eyes. He had seen men die before, but he had never been the cause of it. It was like breaking his Hippocratic oath.

"Some must die," Pearce whispered. "It is better for the evil to die young."

Harry stripped quickly and got into the squire's clothes and goggles. He strapped the pistol down on his hip and turned to Christopher and Pearce. "What about you?"

"We won't try to escape," Pearce said.

"I don't mean that. Will you be all right?"

Pearce put a hand on the boy's shoulder. "Christopher will take care of me. And he will find you after you have rescued Marna."

The confidence in Pearce's voice strengthened Harry. He did not pause to question that confidence. He mounted the motorcycle, settled himself into the saddle seat, and turned the throttle. The motorcycle took off violently.

It was tricky, riding on one wheel, but he had had experience on similar vehicles in the subterranean Medical Center thoroughfares.

His arm hurt, but it was not like it had been before when he was helpless. Now it was a guidance system. As he rode, he could feel the pain lessen. That meant he was getting closer to Marna.

It was night before he found her. The other motorcycles had completely outdistanced him, and he had swept past the side road several miles before the worsening pain warned him. He cruised back and forth before he finally located the curving ramp that led across the cloverleaf ten miles east of Lawrence.

From this a ruined asphalt road turned east, and the pain in Harry's arm had dropped to an ache. The road ended in an impenetrable thicket. Harry stopped just before he crashed into it. He sat immobile on the seat, thinking.

He hadn't considered what he was going to do when he found Marna; he had merely taken off in hot pursuit, driven partly by the painful bracelet on his wrist, partly by his emotional involvement with the girl.

Somehow—he could scarcely trace back the involutions of chance to its source—he had been trapped into leading this pitiful expedition from the Medical Center to the Governor's mansion. Moment by moment it had threatened his life—and not, unless all his hopes were false, just a few years but eternity. Was he going to throw it away here on a quixotic attempt to rescue a girl from the midst of a pack of cruel young wolves?

But what would he do with the thing on his wrist? What of the Governor? And what of Marna?

"Ralph?" someone asked out of the darkness, and the decision was taken out of his hands.

"Yeth," he lipsed. "Where ith everybody?"

"Usual place—under the bank."

Harry moved toward the voice, limping. "Can't thee a thing."

"Here's a light."

The trees lighted up, and a black form loomed in front of Harry. Harry blinked once, squinted, and hit the squire with the edge of his palm on the fourth cervical vertebra. As the man dropped, Harry picked the everlight out of the air, and caught the body. He eased the limp form into the grass and felt the neck. It was broken, but the squire was still breathing. He straightened the head so that there would be no pressure on nerve tissue, and looked up.

Light glimmered and flickered somewhere ahead. There was no movement, no sound; apparently no one had heard him. He flicked the light on, saw the path, and started through the young forest.

The campfire was built under a clay overhang so that it could not be seen from above. Roasting over it was a whole young deer being slowly turned on a spit by one of the squires. Harry found time to recognize the empty ache in his midriff for what it was: hunger.

The rest of the squires sat in a semicircle around the fire. Marna was seated on the far side, her hands bound behind her. Her head was raised; her eyes searched the darkness around the fire. What was she looking for? Of course—for him. She knew by the bracelet on her wrist that he was near.

He wished that he could signal her, but there was no way. He studied the squires: one was an albino; a second, a macrocephalic; a third, a spastic. The others may have had physical impairments that Harry could not see—all except one, who seemed older than the rest and leaned against the edge of the clay bank. He was blind, but inserted surgically into his eye sockets were electrically operated binoculars. He carried a power pack on his back with leads to the binoculars and to an antenna in his coat.

Harry edged cautiously around the forest edge beyond the firelight toward where Marna was sitting.

"First the feast," the albino gloated, "then the fun."

The one who was turning the spit said, "I think we should have the fun first—then we'll be good and hungry."

They argued back and forth, good-naturedly for a moment and then, as others chimed in, with more heat. Finally the albino turned to the one with the binoculars. "What do you say, Eyes?"

In a deep voice, Eyes said, "Sell the girl. Young parts are worth top prices."

"Ah," said the albino slyly, "but you can't see what a pretty little thing she is, Eyes. To you she's only a pattern of white dots against a gray kinescope. To us she's white and pink and black and—"

"One of these days," Eyes said in a calm voice, "you'll go too far."

"Not with her, I won't—"

A stick broke under Harry's foot. Everyone stopped talking and listened. Harry eased his pistol out of its holster.

"Is that you, Ralph?" the albino said.

"Yeth," Harry said, limping out into the edge of the firelight, but keeping his head in the darkness, his pistol concealed at his side.

"Can you imagine?" the albino said. "The girl says she's the Governor's daughter."

"I am," Marna said clearly. "He will have you cut to pieces slowly for what you are going to do."

"But I'm the Governor, dearie," said the albino in a falsetto, "and I don't give a—"

Eyes interrupted, "That's not Ralph. His leg's all right."

Harry cursed his luck. The binoculars were equipped to pick up X-ray reflections as well as radar. "Run!" he shouted in the silence that followed.

His first shot was for Eyes. The man was turning so that it struck his power pack. He began screaming and clawing at the binoculars that served him for eyes. But Harry wasn't watching. He was releasing the entire magazine into the clay bank above the fire. Already loosened by the heat from the fire, the bank collapsed, smothering the fire and burying several of the squires sitting close to it.

Harry dived to the side. Several bullets went through the space he had just vacated.

He scrambled for the forest and started running. He kept slamming into trees, but he picked himself up and ran again. Somewhere he lost his everlight. Behind, the pursuit thinned and died away.

He ran into something that yielded before him. It fell to the ground, something soft and warm. He tripped over it and toppled, his fist drawn back.

"Harry!" Marna said.

His fist turned into a hand that went out to her, pulled her tight. "Marna!" he sobbed. "I didn't know. I didn't think I could do it. I thought you were—"

Their bracelets clinked together. Marna, who had been soft beneath him, suddenly stiffened, pushed him off. "Let's not get slobbery about it," she said angrily. "I know why you did it. Besides, they'll hear us."

Harry drew a quick, outraged breath and then let it come out in a sigh. What was the use? She'd never believe him—why should she? He wasn't sure himself. Now that it was over and he had time to realize the risks he had taken, he began to shiver. He sat there in the dark forest, his eyes closed, and tried to control his shaking.

Marna put her hand out hesitantly and touched his arm. She started to say something, stopped, and the moment was past.

"B-b-brat-t-t!" he chattered. "N-n-nasty—un-ungrate-ful b-b-brat!" And then the shakes were gone.

She started to move. "Sit still!" he whispered. "We've got to wait until they give up the search."

At least he had eliminated the greatest danger: Eyes with his radar, X-ray vision that was just as good by night as by day.

They sat in the darkness and waited, listening to the forest noises. An hour passed. Harry was going to say that perhaps it was safe to move, when he heard something rustling nearby. Animal or human enemy? Marna, who had not touched him again or spoken, clutched his upper arm with a panic-strengthened hand. Harry doubled his fist and drew back his arm.

"Dr. Elliott?" Christopher whispered. "Marna?"

Relief surged over Harry like a warm, life-giving current. "You wonderful little imp! How did you find us?"

"Grampa helped me. He has a sense for that. I have a little, but he's better. Come." Harry felt a small hand fit itself into his.

Christopher began to lead them through the darkness. At first Harry was distrustful, and then, as the boy kept them out of bushes and trees, he moved more confidently. The hand became something he could trust. He knew how Pearce felt, and how bereft he must be now.

Christopher led them a long way before they reached another clearing. A bed of coals glowed dimly beneath a sheltering bower of green leaves. Pearce sat near the fire, slowly turning a spit fashioned from a green branch. It rested on two forked sticks. On the spit two skinned rabbits were golden brown and sizzling.

Pearce's sightless face turned as they entered the clearing. "Welcome back," he said.

Harry felt a warmth inside him that was like coming home. "Thanks," he said huskily.

Marna fell to her knees in front of the fire, raising her hands to it to warm them. Rope dangled from them, frayed in the center where she had methodically picked it apart while she had waited by another fire. She must have been cold, Harry thought, and I let her shiver through the forest while I was warm in my jacket. But there was nothing to say.

When Christopher removed the rabbits from the spit, they almost fell apart. He wrapped four legs in damp green leaves and tucked them away in a cool hollow between two tree roots. "That's for breakfast," he said.

The four of them fell to work on the remainder. Even without salt, it was the most delicious meal Harry had ever eaten. When it was finished, he licked his fingers, sighed, and leaned back on a pile of old leaves. He felt more contented than he could ever remember being. He was a little thirsty, because he had refused to drink from the brook that ran through the woods close to their improvised camp, but he could stand that. A man couldn't surrender all his principles. It would be ironic to die of typhoid so close to his chance at immortality.

That the Governor would confer immortality upon him—or at least put him into a position where he could earn it—he did not doubt. After all, he had saved the Governor's daughter.

Marna was a pretty little thing. It was too bad she was still a child. An alliance with the Governor's family would not hurt his chances. Perhaps in a few years—He put the notion away from him. Marna hated him.

Christopher shoveled dirt over the fire with a large piece of bark. Harry sighed again and stretched luxuriously. Sleeping would be good tonight.

Marna had washed at the brook. Her face was clean and shining. "Will you sleep here beside me?" Harry asked her, touching the dry leaves. He held up his bracelet apologetically. "This thing keeps me awake when you're very far away."

She nodded coldly and sat down beside him—but far enough away so that they did not touch.

Harry said, "I can't understand why we've run across so many teratisms. I can't remember ever seeing one in my practice at the Medical Center."

"You were in the clinics?" Pearce asked. And without waiting for an answer he went on, "Increasingly, the practice of medicine becomes the treatment of monsters. In the city they would die; in the suburbs they are preserved to perpetuate themselves. Let me look at your arm."

Harry started. Pearce had said it so naturally that for a moment he had forgotten that the old man couldn't see. The old man's gentle fingers untied the bandage and carefully pulled the matted grass away. "You won't need this any more."

Harry put his hand wonderingly to the wound. It had not hurt for hours. Now it was only a scar. "Perhaps you really were a doctor. Why did you give up practice?"

Pearce whispered, "I grew tired of being a technician. Medicine had become so desperately complicated that the relationship between doctor and patient was not much different from that between mechanic and patient."

Harry objected: "A doctor has to preserve his distance. If he keeps caring, he won't survive. He must become callous to suffering, inured to sorrow, or he couldn't continue in a calling so intimately associated with them."

"No one ever said," Pearce whispered, "that it was an easy thing to be a doctor. If he stops caring, he loses not only his patient but his own humanity. But the complication of medicine had another effect. It restricted treatment to those who could afford it. Fewer and fewer people grew healthier and healthier. Weren't the rest human, too?"

Harry frowned. "Certainly. But it was the wealthy contributors and the foundations that made it all possible. They had to be treated first so that medical research could continue."

Pearce whispered, "And so society was warped all out of shape; everything was sacrificed to the god of medicine—all so that a few people could live a few years longer. Who paid the bill?

"And the odd outcome was that those who received care grew less healthy, as a class, than those who had to survive without it. Premies were saved to reproduce their weaknesses. Faults that would have proved fatal in childhood were repaired so that the patient reached maturity. Non-survival traits were passed on. Physiological inadequates multiplied, requiring greater care—"

Harry sat upright. "What kind of medical ethics are those? Medicine can't count the cost or weigh the value. Its business is to treat the sick—"

"Those who can afford it. If medicine doesn't evaluate, then someone else will: power or money or groups. One day I walked out on all that. I went among the citizens, where the future was, where I could help without discrimination. They took me in; they fed me when I was hungry, laughed with me when I was happy, cried with me when I was sad. They cared, and I helped them as I could."

"How?" Harry asked. "Without a diagnostic machine, without drugs or antibiotics."

"The human mind," Pearce whispered, "is still the best diagnostic machine. And the best antibiotic. I touched them. I helped them to cure themselves. So I became a healer instead of a technician. Our bodies want to heal themselves, you know, but our minds give counter-orders and death-instructions."

"Witch doctor!" Harry said scornfully.

"Yes. Always there have been witch doctors. Healers. Only in my day have the healer and the doctor become two persons. In every other era the people with the healing touch were the doctors. They existed then; they exist now. Countless cures are testimony. Only today do we call it superstition. And yet we know that some doctors, no wiser or more expert than others, have a far greater recovery rate. Some nurses—not always the most beautiful ones—inspire in their patients a desire to get well.

"It takes you two hours to do a thorough examination; I can do it in two seconds. It may take you months or years to complete a treatment; I've never taken longer than five minutes."

"But where's your control?" Harry demanded. "How can you prove you've helped them? If you can't trace cause and effect, if no one else can duplicate your treatment, it isn't science. It can't be taught."

"When a healer is successful, he knows," Pearce whispered. "So does his patient. As for teaching—how do you teach a child to talk?"

Harry shrugged impatiently. Pearce had an answer for everything. There are people like that, so secure in their mania that they can never be convinced that the rest of the world is sane. Man had to depend on science—not on superstition, not on faith healers, not on miracle workers. Or else he was back in the Dark Ages.

He lay back in the bed of leaves, feeling Marna's presence close to him. He wanted to reach out and touch her, but he didn't.

Else there would be no law, no security, no immortality. . . .

The bracelet awoke him. It tingled. Then it began to hurt. Harry put out his hand. The bed of leaves beside him was warm, but Marna was gone.

"Marna!" he whispered. He raised himself on one elbow. In the starlight that filtered through the trees above, he could just make out that the clearing was empty of everyone but himself. The places where Pearce and the boy had been sleeping were empty. "Where is everybody?" he said, more loudly.

He cursed under his breath. They had picked their time and escaped. But why, then, had Christopher found them in the forest and brought them here? And what did Marna hope to gain? Make it to the mansion alone?

He started up. Something crunched in the leaves. Harry froze in that position. A moment later he was blinded by a brilliant light.

"Don't move!" said a high-pitched voice. "I will have to shoot you. And if you try to dodge, the Snooper will follow." The voice was cool and precise. The hand that held the gun, Harry thought, would be as cool and accurate as the voice.

"I'm not moving," Harry said. "Who are you?"

The voice ignored him. "There were four of you. Where are the other three?"

"They heard you coming. They're hanging back, waiting to rush you."

"You're lying," the voice said contemptuously.

"Listen to me!" Harry said urgently. "You don't sound like a citizen. I'm a doctor—ask me a question about medicine, anything at all. I'm on an urgent mission. I'm taking a message to the Governor."

"What is the message?"

Harry swallowed hard. "The shipment was hijacked. There won't be another ready for a week."

"What shipment?"

"I don't know. If you're a squire, you've got to help me."

"Sit down." Harry sat down. "I have a message for you. Your message won't be delivered."

"But—" Harry started up.

From somewhere behind the light came a small explosion— little more than a sharply expelled breath. Something stung Harry in the chest. He looked down. A tiny dart clung there between the edges of his jacket. He tried to reach for it and couldn't. His arm wouldn't move. His head wouldn't move either. He toppled over onto his side, not feeling the impact. Only his eyes, his ears, and his lungs seemed unaffected. He lay there, paralyzed, his mind racing.

"Yes," the voice said calmly, "I am a ghoul. Some of my friends are head-hunters, but I hunt bodies and bring them in alive. The sport is greater. So is the profit. Heads are worth only twenty dollars; bodies are worth more than a hundred. Some with young organs like yours are worth much more.

"Go, Snooper. Find the others."

The light went away. Something crackled in the brush and was gone. Slowly Harry made out a black shape that seemed to be sitting on the ground about ten feet away.

"You wonder what will happen to you," the ghoul said. "As soon as I find your companions, I will paralyze them, too, and summon my stretchers. They will carry you to my helicopter. Then, since you came from Kansas City, I will take you to Topeka."

A last hope died in Harry's chest.

"That works best, I've found," the high-pitched voice continued. "Avoids complications. The Topeka hospital I do business with will buy your bodies, no questions asked. You are permanently paralyzed, so you will never feel any pain, although you will not lose consciousness. That way the organs never deteriorate. If you're a doctor, as you said, you know what I mean. You may know the technical name for the poison in the dart; all I know is that it was synthesized from the poison of the digger wasp. By use of intravenous feeding, these eminently portable organ banks have been kept alive for years until their time comes. . . ."

The voice went on, but Harry didn't listen. He was thinking that he would go mad. They often did. He had seen them lying on slabs in the organ bank, and their eyes had been quite mad. Then he had told himself that the madness was why they had been put there, but now he knew the truth. He would soon be one of them.

Perhaps he would strangle before he reached the hospital, before they got the tube down his throat and the artificial respirator on his chest and the tubes into his arms. They strangled sometimes, even under care.

He would not go mad, though. He was too sane. He might last for months.

He heard something crackle in the brush. Light flashed across his eyes. Something moved. Bodies thrashed. Someone grunted. Someone else yelled. Something went *pouf!* Then the sounds stopped, except for someone panting.

"Harry!" Marna said anxiously. "Harry! Are you all right?"

The light came back as the squat Snooper shuffled into the little clearing again. Pearce moved painfully through the light. Beyond him was Christopher and Marna. On the ground near them was a twisted creature. Harry couldn't figure out what it was, and then he realized it was a dwarf, a gnome, a man with thin, little legs and a twisted back and a large, lumpy head. Black hair grew sparsely on top of the head, and the eyes looked out redly, hating the world.

"Harry!" Marna said again, a wail this time.

He didn't answer. He couldn't. It was a momentary flash of

pleasure, not being able to answer, and then it was buried in a flood of self-pity.

Marna picked up the dart gun and threw it deep into the brush. "What a filthy weapon!"

Reason returned to Harry. They had not escaped after all. Just as he had told the ghoul, they had only faded away so that they could rescue him if an opportunity came. But they had returned too late.

The paralysis was permanent; there was no antidote. Perhaps they would kill him. How could he make them understand that he wanted to be killed?

He blinked his eyes rapidly.

Marna had moved to him. She cradled his head in her lap. Her hand moved restlessly, smoothing his hair.

Carefully, Pearce removed the dart from his chest and shoved it deep into the ground. "Be calm," he said. "Don't give up. There is no such thing as permanent paralysis. If you will try, you can move your little finger." He held up Harry's hand, patted it.

Harry tried to move his finger, but it was useless. What was the matter with the old quack? Why didn't he kill him and get it over with? Pearce kept talking, but Harry did not listen. What was the use of hoping? It only made the pain worse.

"A transfusion might help," Marna said.

"Yes," Pearce agreed. "Are you willing?"

"You know what I am?"

"Of course. Christopher, search the ghoul. He will have tubing and needles on him for emergency treatment of his victims." Pearce spoke to Marna again. "There will be some commingling. The poison will enter your body."

Marna's voice was bitter. "You couldn't hurt me with cyanide."

There were movements and preparations. Harry couldn't concentrate on them. Things blurred. Time passed like the slow movement of a glacier.

As the first gray light of morning came through the trees, Harry felt life moving painfully in his little finger. It was worse than anything he had ever experienced, a hundred times worse than the pain from the bracelet. The pain spread to his other fingers, to his feet, up his legs and arms toward his trunk. He wanted to plead with Pearce to restore the paralysis, but by the time his throat relaxed, the pain was almost gone.

When he could sit up, he looked around for Marna. She was leaning back against a tree trunk, her eyes closed, looking paler than ever. "Marna!" he said. Her eyes opened wearily; an expression of joy flashed across them as they focused on him, and then they clouded.

"I'm all right," she said.

Harry scratched his left elbow where the needle had been. "I don't understand—you and Pearce—you brought me back from that—but—"

"Don't try to understand," she said. "Just accept it."

"It's impossible," he muttered. "What are you?"

"The Governor's daughter."

"What else?"

"A Cartwright," she said bitterly.

His mind recoiled. One of the Immortals! He was not surprised that her blood had counteracted the poison. Cartwright blood was specific against any foreign substance. He thought of something. "How old are you?"

"Seventeen," she said. She looked down at her slim figure. "We mature late, we Cartwrights. That's why Weaver sent me to the Medical Center—to see if I was fertile. A fertile Cartwright can waste no breeding time."

There was no doubt: she hated her father. She called him Weaver. "He will have you bred," Harry repeated stupidly.

"He will try to do it himself," she said without emotion. "He is not very fertile; that is why there are only three of us—my grandmother, my mother, and me. Then we have some control over conception—particularly after maturity. We don't want his children, even though they might make him less dependent on us. I'm afraid"—her voice broke—"I'm afraid I'm not mature enough."

"Why didn't you tell me before?" Harry demanded.

"And have you treat me like a Cartwright?" Her eyes glowed with anger. "A Cartwright isn't a person, you know. A Cartwright is a walking blood bank, a living fountain of youth, something to be possessed, used, guarded, but never really allowed to live. Besides"—her head dropped—"you don't believe me. About Weaver."

"But he's the Governor!" Harry exclaimed. He saw her face and turned away. How could he explain? You had a job and you had a duty. You couldn't go back on those. And then there were the bracelets. Only the Governor had the key. They couldn't go on for long linked together like that. They would be separated again, by chance or by force, and he would die.

He got to his feet. The forest reeled for a moment, and then settled back. "I owe you thanks again," he said to Pearce.

"You fought hard to preserve your beliefs," Pearce whispered, "but there was a core of sanity that fought with me, that said it was better to be a whole man with crippled beliefs than a crippled man with whole beliefs."

Harry stared soberly at the old man. He was either a real healer who could not explain how he worked his miracles, or the world was a far crazier place than Harry had ever imagined. "If we start moving now," he said, "we should be in sight of the mansion by noon."

As he passed the dwarf, he looked down, stopped, and looked back at Marna and Pearce. Then he stooped, picked up the misshapen little body, and walked toward the road.

The helicopter was beside the turnpike. "It would be only a few minutes if we flew," he muttered.

Close behind him Marna said, "We aren't expected. We would be shot down before we got within five miles."

Harry strapped the dwarf into the helicopter seat. The ghoul stared at him out of hate-filled eyes. Harry started the motor, pressed the button on the autopilot marked "Return," and stepped back. The helicopter lifted, straightened, and headed southeast.

Christopher and Pearce were waiting on the pavement when Harry turned. Christopher grinned suddenly and held out a rabbit leg. "Here's breakfast."

They marched down the turnpike toward Lawrence.

The Governor's mansion was built on the top of an L-shaped hill that stood tall between two river valleys. Once it had been the site of a great university, but taxes for supporting such institutions had been diverted into more vital channels. Private contributions had dwindled as the demands of medical research and medical care had intensified. Soon there was no interest in educational fripperies, and the university died.

The Governor had built his mansion there some seventy-five years ago when Topeka became unbearable. Long before that it had become a lifetime office—and the Governor would live forever.

The state of Kansas was a barony—a description that would have meant nothing to Harry, whose knowledge of history was limited to the history of medicine. The Governor was a baron, and the mansion was his keep. His vassals were the suburban squires; they were paid with immortality or its promise. Once one of them had received an injection, he had two choices: remain loyal to the Governor and live forever, barring accidental death, or grow old again within thirty days.

The Governor had not received a shipment for four weeks. The squires were getting desperate.

The mansion was a fortress. Its outer walls were five-foot-thick pre-stressed concrete faced with five-inch armor plate. A moat surrounded the walls; it was stocked with piranha.

An inner wall rose above the outside one. The paved, unencumbered area between the two could be flooded with napalm. Inside the wall were hidden guided-missile nests.

The mansion rose, ziggurat fashion, in terraced steps. On each rooftop was a hydroponic farm. At the summit of the buildings was a glass penthouse; the noon sun turned it into silver. On a mast towering above, a radar dish rotated.

Like an iceberg, most of the mansion was beneath the surface. It went down through limestone and granite a mile deep. The building was almost a living creature; automatic mechanisms controlled it, brought in air, heated and cooled it, fed it, watered it, watched for enemies and killed them if they got too close. . . .

It could be run by a single hand. At the moment it was.

There was no entrance to the place. Harry stood in front of the walls and waved his jacket. "Ahoy, the mansion! A message for the Governor from the Medical Center. Ahoy, the mansion!"

"Down!" Christopher shouted.

An angry bee buzzed past Harry's ear and then a whole flight of them. Harry fell to the ground and rolled. In a little while the bees stopped.

"Are you hurt?" Marna asked quickly.

Harry lifted his face out of the dust. "Poor shots," he said grimly. "Where did they come from?"

"One of the villas," Christopher said, pointing at the scattered dwellings at the foot of the hill.

"The bounty wouldn't even keep them in ammunition," Harry said.

In a giant, godlike voice, the mansion spoke: "Who comes with a message for me?"

Harry shouted from his prone position, "Dr. Harry Elliott. I have with me the Governor's daughter Marna and a leech. We're under fire from one of the villas."

The mansion was silent. Slowly then a section of the inside wall swung open. Something flashed into the sunlight, spurting flame from its tail. It darted downward. A moment later a villa lifted into the air and fell back, a mass of rubble.

Over the outer wall came a crane arm. From it dangled a large metal car. When it reached the ground a door opened.

"Come into my presence," the mansion said.

The car was dusty. So was the penthouse where they were deposited. The vast swimming pool was dry; the cabanas were rotten; the flowers and bushes and palm trees were dead.

In the mirror-surfaced central column, a door gaped at them like a dark mouth. "Enter," said the door.

The elevator descended deep into the ground. Harry's stomach surged uneasily; he thought the car would never stop, but eventually the doors opened. Beyond was a spacious living room, decorated in shades of brown. One entire wall was a vision screen.

Marna ran out of the car. "Mother!" she shouted. "Grandmother!" She raced through the apartment. Harry followed her more slowly.

There were six bedrooms opening off a long hall. At the end of it was a nursery. On the other side of the living room were a dining room and a kitchen. Every room had a wall-wide vision screen. Every room was empty.

"Mother?" Marna said again.

The dining-room screen flickered. Across the huge screen flowed the giant image of a creature who lolled on pneumatic cushions. It was a thing incredibly fat, a sea of flesh rippling and surging. Although it was naked, its sex was a mystery. The breasts were great pillows of fat, but there was a sprinkling of hair between them. Its face, moon though it was, was small on the fantastic body; in it eyes were stuck like raisins.

It drew sustenance out of a tube; then, as it saw them, it pushed the tube away with one balloonlike hand. It giggled; the giggle was godlike.

"Hello, Marna," it said in the mansion's voice. "Looking for somebody? Your mother and your grandmother thwarted me, you know. Sterile creatures! I connected them directly to the blood bank; now there will be no delay about blood—"

"You'll kill them!" Marna gasped.

"Cartwrights? Silly girl! Besides, this is our bridal night, and we would not want them around, would we, Marna?"

Marna shrank back into the living room, but the creature looked at her from that screen, too. It turned its raisin eyes toward Harry. "You are the doctor with the message. Tell me."

Harry frowned. "You—are Governor Weaver?"

"In the flesh, boy." The creature chuckled. It made waves of fat surge across its body and back again.

Harry took a deep breath. "The shipment was hijacked. It will be a week before another shipment is ready."

Weaver frowned and reached a stubby finger toward something beyond the camera's range. "There!" He looked back at Harry and smiled the smile of an idiot. "I just blew up Dean Mock's office. He was inside it at the time. It's justice, though. He's been sneaking shots of elixir for twenty years."

"Elixir? But—!" The information about Mock was too unreal to be meaningful; Harry didn't believe it. It was the mention of elixir that shocked him.

Weaver's mouth made an "O" of sympathy. "I've shocked you. They tell you the elixir has not been synthesized. It was. Some one hundred years ago by a doctor named Russell Pearce. You were planning on synthesizing it, perhaps, and thereby winning yourself immortality as a reward. No—I'm not telepathic. Fifty out of every one hundred doctors dream that dream. I'll tell you, doctor—I am the electorate. I decide who shall be immortal, and it pleases me to be arbitrary. Gods are always arbitrary. That is what makes them gods. I could give you immortality. I will; I will. Serve me well, doctor, and when you begin to age, I will make you young again. I could make you dean of the Medical Center. Would you like that?"

Weaver frowned again. "But no—you would sneak elixir, like Mock, and you would not send me the shipment when I need it for my squires." He scratched between his breasts. "What will I do?" He wailed. "The loyal ones are dying off. I can't give them their shots, and then their children are ambushing their parents. Whitey crept up on his father the other day; sold him to a junk collector. Old hands keep young hands away from the fire. But the old ones are dying off, and the young ones don't need the elixir, not yet. They will, though. They'll come to me on their knees, begging, and I'll laugh at them and let them die. That's what gods do, you know."

Weaver scratched his wrist. "You're still shocked about the elixir. You think we should make gallons of it, keep everybody young forever. Now think about it! We know that's absurd, eh? There wouldn't be enough of anything to go around. And what would be the value of immortality if everybody lived forever?" His voice changed suddenly, became businesslike. "Who hijacked the shipment? Was it this man?"

A picture flashed on the lower quarter of the screen.

"Yes," Harry said. His brain was spinning. Illumination and immortality, all in one breath. It was coming too fast. He didn't have time to react.

Weaver rubbed his doughy mouth. "Cartwright! How can he do it?" There was a note of godlike fear in the voice. "To risk—forever. He's mad—that's it, the man is mad. He wants to die." The great mass of flesh shivered; the body rippled. "Let him try me. I'll give him death." He looked at Harry again and scratched his neck. "How did you get here, you four?"

"We walked," Harry said tightly.

"Walked? Fantastic!"

"Ask a motel manager just this side of Kansas City, or a pack of wolves that almost got away with Marna, or a ghoul that paralyzed me. They'll tell you we walked."

Weaver scratched his mountainous belly. "Those wolf packs.

They can be a nuisance. They're useful, though. They keep the countryside tidy. But if you were paralyzed, why is it you are here instead of waiting to be put to use on some organ-bank slab?"

"The leech gave me a transfusion from Marna." Too late Harry saw Marna motioning for him to be silent.

Weaver's face clouded. "You've stolen my blood! Now I can't bleed her for a month. I will have to punish you. Not now, but later when I have thought of something fitting the crime."

"A month is too soon," Harry said. "No wonder the girl is pale if you bleed her every month. You'll kill her."

"But she's a Cartwright," Weaver said in astonishment, "and I need the blood."

Harry's lips tightened. He held up the bracelet on his wrist. "The key, sir?"

"Tell me," Weaver said, scratching under one breast, "is Marna fertile?"

"No, sir." Harry looked levelly into the eyes of the Governor of Kansas. "The key?"

"Oh, dear," Weaver said. "I seem to have misplaced it. You'll have to wear the bracelets yet a bit. Well, Marna. We will see how it goes tonight, eh, fertile or no? Find something suitable for a bridal night, will you? And let us not mar the occasion with weeping and moaning and screams of pain. Come reverently and filled with a great joy, as Mary came unto God."

"If I have a child," Marna said, her face white, "it will have to be a virgin birth."

The sea of flesh surged with anger. "Perhaps there will be screams tonight. Yes. Leech! You—the obscenely old person with the boy. You are a healer."

"So I have been called," Pearce whispered.

"They say you work miracles. Well, I have a miracle for you to work." Weaver scratched the back of one hand. "I itch. Doctors have found nothing wrong with me, and they have died. It drives me mad."

"I cure by touch," Pearce said. "Every person cures himself; I only help."

"No man touches me," Weaver said. "You will cure me by tonight. I will not hear of anything else. Otherwise I will be angry with you and the boy. Yes, I will be very angry with the boy if you do not succeed."

"Tonight," Pearce said, "I will work a miracle for you."

Weaver smiled and reached out for a feeding tube. His dark eyes glittered like black marbles in a huge dish of custard. "Tonight, then!" The image vanished from the screen.

"A grub," Harry whispered. "A giant white grub in the heart of a rose. Eating away at it, blind, selfish, and destructive."

"I think of him," Pearce said, "as a fetus who refuses to be born. Safe in the womb, he destroys the mother, not realizing that he is thereby destroying himself." He turned slightly toward Christopher. "There is an eye?"

Christopher looked at the screen. "Every one."

"Bugs."

"All over."

Pearce said, "We will have to take the chance that he will not audit the recordings, or that he can be distracted long enough to do what must be done."

Harry looked at Marna and then at Pearce and Christopher. "What can we do?"

"You're willing?" Marna said. "To give up immortality? To risk everything?"

Harry grimaced. "What would I be losing? A world like this—"

"What is the situation?" Pearce whispered. "Where is Weaver?"

Marna shrugged helplessly. "I don't know. My mother and grandmother never knew. He sends the elevator. There are no stairs, no other exits. And the elevators are controlled from a console beside his bed. There are thousands of switches. They also control the rest of the building, the lights, water, air, heat, and food supplies. He can release toxic or anesthetic gases or flaming gasoline. He can set off charges not only here but in Topeka and Kansas City, or send rockets to attack other areas. There's no way to reach him."

"You will reach him," Pearce whispered.

Marna's eyes lighted up. "If there were some weapon I could take—But there's an inspection in the elevator—magnetic and fluoroscopic detectors."

"Even if you could smuggle in a knife, say," Harry said, frowning, "it would be almost impossible to hit a vital organ. And even though he isn't able to move his body, his arms must be fantastically strong."

"There is, perhaps, one way," Pearce said. "If we can find a piece of paper, Christopher will write it out for you."

The bride waited near the elevator doors. She was dressed in white satin and old lace. The lace was pulled up over the head for a veil. In front of the living-room screen, in a brown velour Grand Rapids overstuffed chair, sat Pearce. At his feet, leaning against his bony knee, was Christopher.

The screen flickered, and Weaver was there, grinning his divine-idiot's grin. "You're impatient, Marna. It pleases me to see you so eager to rush into the arms of your bridegroom. The wedding carriage arrives."

The doors of the elevator sighed open. The bride stepped into the car. As the doors began to close, Pearce got to his feet, pushing Christopher gently to one side, and said, "You seek immortality, Weaver, and you think you have found it. But what you have is only a living death. I am going to show you the only real immortality. . . ."

The car dropped. It plummeted to the tune of the wedding march from Lohengrin. Detectors probed at the bride and found only cloth. The elevator began to slow. After it came to a full stop, the doors remained closed for a moment, and then, squeaking, they opened.

The stench of decay flowed into the car. For a moment the

bride recoiled, and then stepped forward out of the car. The room had once been a marvelous mechanism: a stainless steel womb. Not much bigger than the giant pneumatic mattress that occupied the center, the room was completely automatic. Temperature regulators kept it at blood heat. Food came directly from the processing rooms through the tubes without human aid. Sprays had been installed for water to sweep dirt and refuse to collectors around the edge of the room that would dispose of it. An overhead spray was to wash the creature who occupied the mattress. Around the edges of the mattress, like a great circular organ with ten thousand keys, was a complex control console. Directly over the mattress, on the ceiling, was a view screen.

Some years before, apparently, a waterpipe had broken, through some shift in the earth, and a small leak or a hard freeze had made the rock swell. The cleansing sprays no longer worked, and the occupant of the room either was afraid to have intruders trace the trouble, or he no longer cared.

The floor was littered with decaying food, with cans and wrappers, with waste matter. As the bride stepped into the room a multitude of cockroaches scattered. Mice scampered into hiding places.

The bride pulled the long white-satin skirt up above her hips. She unwound a thin, nylon cord from her waist. There was a loop fastened into the end. She shook it out until it hung free.

She had seen that Weaver was watching the overhead screen with almost hypnotic concentration. Pearce was talking. "Aging is not a physical disease; it is mental. The mind grows tired and lets the body die. Only half the Cartwrights' immunity to death lies in their blood; the other half is their unflagging will to live.

"You are one hundred and fifty-three years old. I tended your father, who died before you were born. I gave him, unwittingly, a transfusion of Marshall Cartwright's blood."

Weaver whispered, "But that would make you—" His voice was thin and high; it was not godlike at all. It was ridiculous coming from that vast mass of flesh.

"Almost two hundred years old," Pearce said. His voice was stronger, richer, deeper—no longer a whisper. "Without ever a transfusion of Cartwright blood, ever an injection of the *elixir vitae.* The effective mind can achieve conscious control of the autonomic nervous system, of the very cells that make up the blood stream and the body."

The bride craned her neck to see the screen on the ceiling. Pearce looked odd. He was taller. His legs were straight and muscular. His shoulders were broader. As the bride watched, muscle and flesh and fat built up beneath his skin, firming it, smoothing out wrinkles. The facial bones receded beneath young flesh and skin. Silky white hair seemed to thicken and grow darker, although that was impossible.

"You wonder why I stayed old," Pearce said, and his voice was resonant and powerful. "It is something one does not use for oneself. It comes through giving, not taking."

His sunken eyelids grew full, paled, opened. And Pearce looked out at Weaver, tall, strong, and straight—no more than thirty, surely. There was power latent in that face—power leashed, under control. Weaver recoiled from it.

Then, onto the screen, walked Marna.

Weaver's eyes bulged. His head swiveled toward the bride. Harry tossed off the veil and swung the looped cord lightly between two fingers. The importance of his next move was terrifying. The first throw had to be accurate, because he might never have a chance for another. His surgeon's fingers were deft, but he had never thrown a lariat. Christopher had described how he should do it, but there had been no chance to practice.

And if he were dragged within reach of those doughy arms! A hug would smother him.

And in that startled moment, Weaver's head lifted with surprise and his hand stabbed toward the console. Harry flipped the cord. The loop dropped over Weaver's head and tightened around his neck.

Quickly Harry wrapped the cord several times around his hand

and pulled it tight. Weaver jerked against it, tightening it further. The thin cord disappeared into the neck's soft flesh. Weaver's stubby fingers clawed at it, tearing the skin, as his body thrashed on the mattress.

He had, Harry thought crazily, an Immortal at the end of his fishing line—a great white whale struggling to free itself so that it could live forever, smacking the pneumatic waves with fierce lunges and savage tugs. For him it became dreamlike and unreal.

Weaver, by some titanic effort, had turned over. He had his hands around the cord now. He rose onto soft, flowing knees and pulled at the cord, dragging Harry forward toward the mattress. Weaver's eyes were beginning to bulge out of his pudding-face.

Harry dug his heels into the floor. Weaver came up, like the whale leaping its vast bulk incredibly out of the water, and stood, shapeless and monstrous, his face purpling. Then, deep inside, the heart gave up, and the body sagged. It flowed like a melting wax image back to the mattress on which it had spent almost three-quarters of a century.

Harry dazedly unwrapped the cord from his hand. It had cut deep into the skin; blood welled out. He didn't feel anything as he dropped the cord. He shut his eyes and shivered.

After a period of time that he never remembered, he heard someone calling him. "Harry!" It was Marna's voice. "Are you all right? Harry, please!"

He took a deep breath. "Yes. Yes, I'm all right."

"Go to the console," said the young man who had been Pearce. "You'll have to find the right controls, but they should be marked. We've got to release Marna's mother and grandmother. And then we've got to get out of here ourselves. Marshall Cartwright is outside, and I think he's getting impatient."

Harry nodded, but still he waited. It would take a strong man to go out into a world where immortality was a fact rather than a dream. He would have to live with it and its problems. And they would be greater than anything he had imagined.

He moved forward to begin the search.